D1340175

The Black Hole Pastrami

Stories

"There are no extremes in these stories; the sadness is mild and the humor is soft. There's an echo of Jean Shepherd's work here, a humorous and slightly fictionalized recounting of an affectionately-recalled if not perfect childhood and life—instead of a Red Rider BB gun, a young boy carries around a pillow case full of explosives with which to battle Nazis.

IR Verdict: Jeffrey M. Feingold writes with tremendous charm and has a gentle, affectionate attitude towards his characters and their situations in THE BLACK HOLE PASTRAMI, a collection of stories that are quick and comforting reads."

- Indie Reader

"Feingold's collection of short stories approaches themes of childhood, illness, death, and remorse.

Sixteen tales are offered here, many of which examine family relations and Ukrainian Jewish heritage ... Feingold's stories are written in the first person and emotionally have the feel of autobiography. The release captured at the close of "The Black Hole Pastrami" is profoundly moving: "The black hole cracked open; light streamed out. For the first time, I forgave myself. For not saving them. For failing at the impossible." The author is also expert at describing shifting personal perspectives; one regards the aunt who embarrasses her teenage nephew by stealing sugar differently when it's explained that she lived through rationing during the Depression and World War II.

Although Feingold's stories can be darkly poignant, they can also make readers laugh out loud, as when the patient with the tissue graft in "Seventh Sense" announces: "I taste dead people." The collected tales are also intriguing due to the echoes that link them. Further references to The Sixth Sense star Bruce Willis crop up in other stories, as do mentions of the black pastrami, making for delightful moments.

Feingold has a pleasantly unconventional descriptive style, unusually capturing events such as sitting in the dentist's chair: "my mouth as wide open as an angry hippopotamus, as he poked with cold pointy instruments..." a textured, imaginative debut collection. Inventive and emotionally observant writing."

- Kirkus Reviews

"Satisfying and often joyful, these short stories concern family connections and childhood memories.

Jeffrey M. Feingold's endearing short story collection The Black Hole Pastrami compiles memories of growing up in a Jewish household and being a first-generation American.

Each narrator in the collection looks back on their personal history, resulting in an engaging dialogue between the past and the present. The book's warm prose further unifies the collection. A kind, playful tone suffuses the stories, allowing even the darker meditations on death and mortality to seem uplifting and life-affirming.

In "The Black Hole Pastrami," the narrator looks back on his younger self as he buys a pastrami sandwich for his dying father. Rich thoughts spring from this moment in a butcher shop: the man reflects on the aspirations and disappointments he inherited from his father, the unresolved trauma of watching his grandmother die alone, and his inexplicable failure to cry for the deceased members of his family. The sandwich becomes a conduit for connecting with his family and his Jewish Ukrainian roots; through it, he resurrects the tastes and feelings of his childhood.

"The Black Hole Pastrami" is one of several interrelated stories that share a single narrator. With each such entry, facts about and memories of the man's life build up, resulting in complex, detailed depictions of himself and others. In the end, these particular stories are greater than the sum of their parts. Their narrator's emotional development is satisfying, even joyful, even as doubts and questions linger regarding his family relationships, his connection to Judaism, and his visit to the Soviet Union.

Indeed, family, memory, and childhood are the book's recurring themes. Some stories, like "The Buzz Bomb," in which a group of children plays war games every Saturday, are less concerned with ancestral legacies than they are with nostalgia. Indeed, that story recalls the reckless freedom of midcentury childhoods: the narrator carries a sheet holding Roman candles, window shakers, and buzz bombs with him, introducing a grand universe in a short space. The book's longest entry, "Here's Looking at You, Syd," is a comedic account of an American couple's efforts to adopt a child from the Soviet Union.

Quirky, eccentric characters populate the short stories collected in The Black Hole Pastrami."

- *Forward Reviews*

"The stories of Jeffrey M. Feingold's The Black Hole Pastrami are written with an uncommonly deft touch. Feingold knows just when to nudge readers with a metaphorical elbow and when to swing the figurative hammer. These stories are brief but not underdeveloped. Complex but not complicated. Sensitive but not sentimental. Literary but not conventional. Ironic but not sarcastic. Humorous but not jokey. Secretive but not obscure. Character-driven but not plot-impaired. Unpredictable but not random. Feingold pulls off his storytelling balancing act like a tightrope walker who lets us delight in the ultimate performance while barely noticing the years of practice."
- *John Sheirer, author of Stumbling Through Adulthood: Linked Stories*

"At once a love letter to family and an examination of the tension between carefree and careless youth and regretful middle age, this charming collection of stories is full of heart and humor and speaks not only of the lives of its characters but the lives of Eastern European immigrants in America and their children, what their new country made possible in their lives and what it delimited. Each story opens a window into a defining moment in a character's life, and together these moments make up a picture of American lives and immigrant traditions."
– *Christian Livermore, author of We Are Not OK*

"Jeffrey Feingold's story collection, The Black Hole Pastrami, is a delicious offering of interwoven stories, seasoned with surrealism, humor, a bit of regret, a lot of heart. One great benefit of this collection of very short stories is that once you have turned it's every page, you have time to read it again, the second time lingering over your favorites. For me, one of those is the surprisingly poignant story of the child who loses control of the family car in imaginary single-minded, ardent pursuit of Nazis, the length of his legs an unfortunate mismatch to his determination to vanquish the foe and win World War II. Each story has its own turning point, while the collection as a whole is like a Maypole of interconnectedness: relationships and images that reach through several narratives to continually connect and reconnect to remind us that this could as easily be called a novel."
-*Jan Maher, author of Heaven, Indiana and Earth As It Is*

For David and my sisters.

ISBN: 9798388289186

The Black Hole Pastrami

Stories

Jeffrey M. Feingold

Table of Contents

The Black Hole Pastrami

"What's a nice vegetarian boy like you doing in a butcher shop like this?" Howie the butcher asked me as he stood behind his deli counter, adding, "I haven't seen you in here in years."

"My father's dying," I said. "He wants a black pastrami sandwich. He's home now in bed with Itzhak Perlman."

"Izzy—the guy who owns the deli on Morton Avenue?" Howie asked, looking perplexed.

"No, the classical violinist," I said. "My father is home in bed, listening to his favorite records and dying. He asked me to get him a black pastrami on rye, extra mustard. Can you use the good stuff, the whole pastrami?"

Howie seemed stunned, frozen in place, save for his large beefy hands, dripping with chicken fat, which he wiped slowly on his black smock. Between us, inside the glass deli case, sat the largest black pastrami known to man.

Dead animals were everywhere. Parts from cows and chickens, cut or pressed or whole, sat in silver trays running from one end of the long deli case to the other. Whole chickens, cooked, raw, basted, broiled, twirled on strings above, pirouetting in a macabre dance. I wanted to run from the butcher shop fast as I could to find a place to get a hummus and falafel sandwich.

"Come to think of it," Howie said, "I haven't seen your father in here for years either."

As Howie and I were alone in the shop, except for the dancing chickens, I explained my father's absence in recent years. I told him my father had grown up on a diet of eastern European Jewish foods. He was first generation American; his father and mother emigrated to Boston from Ukraine. Pastrami, roast chicken, potato knishes, schmaltz, blintzes, kishke, kugel—these were the foods of my father's formative years.

But about five years ago, shortly after his first cancer diagnosis, my father and mother began cooking together. They became quite the gourmands. Whenever I visited my parents with my now ex-wife, we were treated to a three-star Michelin meal. French dishes, whose names I dared not try to pronounce to my Francophile, French-speaking father; pastries, which I swore my parents must have ascended to heaven to steal from the gods, as it seemed impossible that mere mortals could have baked them; complex wines my father curated, also with names I dared not attempt to pronounce. Gone were the humble European Jewish peasant foods of my father's youth. Gone were his trips to the deli.

Now, as he lay dying, my father wanted to remember the succulent, juicy, peppery-sweet taste of a simple pastrami sandwich.

Howie cut in his slicing machine thin strips of pastrami. The pastrami was crescent shaped, pink middle, outside blackened by pepper as dark as my father's black moon-round eyes.

As Howie worked on the sandwich, I thought about the five years elapsed since my father's initial diagnosis and treatment for cancer, until the current, inoperable, terminal recurrence.

Before today's plan to bring my Dad pastrami, I had tried in those years of remission to bring back other things for him. Both born in Boston, we fished together all-over New England in my early years. Memories of sitting in a little flat bass boat, fishing for small bass or perch or pickerel as the sun rose over open water, are among my favorites. I remember countless ponds and lakes, the still morning air chill but sweet-smelling of spring flowers, water like glass, silver fish darting in and out of lily pads, flashing brief glints of light against the blue morning sky, flashes of light reflecting in the black pools of Dad's eyes.

In the decades since I'd fished with him as a kid, acid rain and other pollutants had killed all the freshwater fish in most New England lakes and ponds. Unless a body of water was stocked, there wasn't a living fish to be had. I felt as if, in waiting too long to fish with him again, I'd failed him. I couldn't bring the past back to life.

Not freshwater fishing.

Nor large family Seders at Passover, when my parent's house was filled with relatives from the old country, speaking Yiddish and Hebrew at the enormous rectangular Seder table, as plates of traditional foods were passed after prayers among smiling happy relatives.

After his first diagnosis, I held a Seder at my house. But, just as that day at the lake, where no fish swam, my Seder was a disappointment to Dad. There was no one there other than Dad who could read the prayers in Hebrew. No one else to remember the family stories told in Yiddish. No one to cook the forgotten recipes from the old country. The past had passed irretrievably.

My efforts always disappointed Dad. Not that he wasn't proud of my accomplishments in life. First generation to go to college. A successful career. A family and children. But my efforts to drive away the sadness I often saw behind his eyes by restoring what was lost were a lost cause.

Dad's losses in life started early. His father came to America from Ukraine and opened a little convenience store. But my father, who loved the stars, had loftier dreams. He planned on college to be an astronomer. He could trace the trail of constellations better than I could trace the trail of freckles on my first girlfriend's face. And I'd studied Molly's face freckles very studiously. Many nights, Dad and I happily peered through his large telescope as he explained stars and constellations and galaxies to me. How stars are born, in unfathomably massive explosions. And how eventually they die, collapsing in on themselves into blackness.

My Dad was born for the stars. But when his mother was sent home to die from cancer, when he was still a young man, before I was born, my father set aside his dreams of college and stardom to work in his Dad's five-and-dime store and help support his family. I always believed these forsaken dreams were behind the sadness in his eyes.

"Nuts!" Howie exclaimed. "I'm out of mustard. I'll just go back to the stockroom to check." He walked into a back room in search of the dark stone-ground mustard he needed to make my Dad's sandwich the old way.

Standing at the deli case, in front of the black pastrami, remembering looking through Dad's telescope as we talked about black holes. Then I remembered how my wife, shortly before we divorced, said I was empty inside, just like a black hole. Was she right? Was something wrong with me? Why couldn't I feel as deeply as she did?

My father, the man of science, loved the original Star Trek television series. Friday nights, 10:00 p.m., the one night of the week I was allowed to stay up that late to watch with him. Spock was my favorite character. The Vulcan who'd learned to control all feeling. He contained it, bottled it, put the closed bottle away deep inside himself. A black hole. This was around the time of my life when I saw my beloved Nana die of a heart attack in front of me at her doctor's office. I decided then, I would be Spock. No tears. That wouldn't be logical. Now, twenty years later, my father was dying. Time to compartmentalize again.

"We're saved!" Howie said, as he walked back behind the deli counter holding a jar of spicy stone-ground mustard he'd retrieved from the stockroom. He removed a large bulkie roll from a plastic bag, sliced it in half, then began making a fat pastrami sandwich. When finished, he wrapped it in crinkly wax paper, along with a Kosher dill pickle. Then slipped it into a brown paper bag.

"Tell your Dad, I'll say a prayer for him," Howie said as I exited the shop.

At my parents' house I sat at the kitchen table with Dad. The pastrami sandwich, cut in half—pink and black and juicy atop the translucent wax paper—was in front of him on the table. After just a few bites, he put it down. He said he couldn't taste it. The chemotherapy caused the food to taste metallic and bitter. I was heartbroken that this, his last chosen meal, was denied him. Just as with fishing and Seders, I was too late.

I didn't cry when my Dad died. I held it in. Put the feelings in an airtight compartment, deep within a place from where no light could escape. I went on with my life. Career, marriage, children. It was a full life.

Then, twenty years after Dad's death, a strange thing happened.

As I sat on the cold exam room floor at my vet, next to my dying Basset Hound, Maggie, watching as the light left her eyes, something changed. I cried for Maggie, for Dad, for Nana, for my broken marriage and for myself. The black hole cracked open; light streamed out. For the first time, I forgave myself. For not saving them. For failing at the impossible. For not saving Nana from her massive heart attack. For not saving my marriage. For not saving my father from his disappointments in life. His failure to become an astronomer. His longing for the past, when lakes teemed with flashing fish, when large family gatherings held traditional Passover Seders, and when a poor boy of Ukrainian stock with star-crossed dreams enjoyed the simple pleasure of the most delicious black whole pastrami on earth.

●

Ahead of me—far ahead—I saw my salvation: a blinking white neon
light, its flashing rays stabbing into the darkness. M-O-T-E-L … M-O-
T-E-L … M-O-T-E-L. I was driving to nowhere, from nowhere. From
one mindless meeting to the next, selling something, I don't remember
what. I had been driving all day and was lost. No GPS and no maps.
Drenching rain poured down on my rental car, a gray Ford something-
or-other, rain pouring so hard it was hard to see down the road. All
day, I'd seen nothing but cornfields. I was tired in my bones. Maybe it's
a Motel 6, I thought, and with their "we'll leave the light on for you"
slogan in my head, I pulled into the empty parking lot of the motel.

In my tiny room there was a bed, a nightstand, and a small television
with rabbit ear antenna. The yellow light from the lamp cast dimly
on the dingy mustard-colored walls. I sat on the edge of the bed, on
a thin mattress resting atop a creaky box spring, and turned the TV
power switch on. Is this it? Is this my whole life? Trudging through
nondescript towns, year after mundane year, selling something to
someone. Bad food, creaky hotel mattresses … drudgery. For years, I'd
been moving forward, focused only on getting ahead in life.

My family had a long history of moving forward. My grandparents
escaped persecution in Ukraine. They fled west, to America. A
perilous journey. They never talked to me about what they left behind.
Perhaps it's why they never kept things. Certainly not things from the
old country. They were always looking ahead, never behind. History,
after all, was a nightmare from which my forebears had struggled to
awaken. They were mostly gone now, my forebears, dead these many
years. So long ago. I hardly ever thought of them. I, too, was moving
forward.

I flicked the TV remote through a few channels. And then it happened.
The Frugal Gourmet show appeared on screen. Jeff Smith, the Frugal
Gourmet, was Scandinavian, as white as a ghost, with a white beard,
a white shirt, and a plate full of white food. He was whiter than the
Ghost of Christmas Past. And little did I know that, as the Christmas

ghost had for frugal Scrooge, the Frugal ghost was about to take me on a strange journey.

Standing next to the Gourmet was the greatest violinist of our generation, Itzhak Perlman. The theme of the rerun episode that day was foods from their youth. Jeff Smith made Lutefisk, a whitefish soaked in lye, and cauliflower with white sauce, and of course white bread. He held a plate of white at an angle for the camera to see. A white-shirted, white-bearded pale ghost with a plate of white. Then it was Itzhak's turn. Itzhak had a huge crop of curly black hair, bushy black sideburns, big glasses, a broad face, a booming baritone voice, and a beaming smile. He was as colorful—in every way—as the Gourmet was white.

"Today, I am going to make a dish I grew up with," he said. "Salami and eggs! First, I drizzle a little of this schmalz in the pan. Schmaltz is chicken fat. It's been a part of traditional Ashkenazi Jewish cooking for centuries."

He poured some of the fat into the pan and it sizzled. I watched intently.

"Now, I'm going to add the salami slices," Itzhak said.

As he added the thin slices to the frying pan, the pan sizzled loudly, and I was struck by a bolt of lightning. I literally couldn't move. I smelled right through the TV a scent I'd forgotten so long ago, as acrid and as real as if I were there standing next to Itzhak. My father loved salami and eggs. When I was a boy, he made it on weekends. Its pungent umami scent was so overpowering it filled my parents' entire house. It smelled to me then like earth, farm animals, barns, pogroms, and like the nightmare of history. And besides, I thought when I was nine or ten, as my Dad fried the noxious stuff in our kitchen, it was just so—grody.

But now, sitting alone on the edge of a bed in some cheap motel, I closed my eyes as Itzhak fried. I was transported to my parents' house. The frying salami had carried me back forty years through time. With my eyes still closed, I saw myself, there with my extended family, gathered around the Passover supper table, laughing and drinking. Somber Jewish melodies from my grandfather's cello filled the dining room, the seder candles flickered in the day's dying light, there were prayers and whispers and jokes in Yiddish. Aunts and uncles, grandparents and great grandparents, sisters, cousins, and family friends sat around the enormous rectangular Seder table as all ate and drank and laughed. Bowls full of matzo ball soup, and plates full of roast chicken, were passed along the table from one smiling relative to another. Aunt Millie threw her arms around me and planted a big wet smooch on my cheek. "Come, sit, I'll make you a plate of chopped liver. Look at you, little one, too thin, eat, eat!" I walked over to my grandfather. He stopped playing cello and looked up at me. His eyes were soulful but bright.

"Where have you been, child?" he asked.

"Nowhere," I replied. "I'm right here," I say. "I never left."

●

Grace

I wanted you to know that if I died that day, you shouldn't grieve too long. I'd lived a bountiful life. Eight years of grace. My years with you.

Driving to your Mom's. Summer morning. Windows open, top down, warm jet stream rustling your yellow hair like a field of dancing mustard.

I wasn't ill. Not pondering death. Although, I thought, dying is the most human thing.

Nor were you ill.

Still, I wanted you to know.

I spoke softly. "Hannah Grace, if your doctor called my cell this moment, to say she was with you in hospital, and that you'd perish unless I got there within five minutes to donate two kidneys, I'd spin this car around and speed to your side faster than a bullet train. No remorse. No regret. The *Kidney Express* would be hurtling down the track to bring two kidneys to you."

You flashed a pearl smile. Blushed cherry blossom cheeks. Wind-tussled hair weaving lithe dancers in the Swan Lake pas de deux. Moist pool-blue eyes revealed. You brushed my arm with your white swan-wing hand. I slipped the black convertible to the roadside for us to watch the rising sun splash yellow paint across a green canvas field.

"Oh, Dad, that's so wonderful." Then, "can I ask you something?"

"Anything," I replied, bracing. Divorce. Disease. Death. Those pool-blue eyes had reflected so much.

I inhaled. Breathless. Iron rod fingers gripping wheel.

"How many kidneys do we have?"

I exhaled. Breathed. Iron fingers melting back into flesh.

"Eight," I whispered, "but my best two are on the way to you the instant that call comes."

I drank black coffee at your Mom's kitchen table. She signed divorce papers. On the porch swing, you read the book of Greek myths I'd given for your eighth birthday. Your beloved Icarus. Book down, you whirled white wax-feather wings as you flew across the green grass field. White wingtips touching blue sky. I sipped black coffee, signed papers, fearing, how, now, can I shield you from the merciless sun?

●

Here's Looking at You, Syd

As my wife, Anna, and her best friend, Ruthie, sat in Ruthie's and her Brit husband Ian's Boston brownstone living room chitchatting, I slumped in a chair in the kitchen, sipping bitter black coffee with Ian, who held up the only three fingers remaining on his right hand, and whispered, "there are just three things you must do to stay alive during your second Russia trip."

Only three, I wondered.

Had Anna secretly told Ian about my Attention Deficit Disorder? What if there were really four or six or even eight things? Eight imperative things to prevent dying hard in any of eight different dreadful ways in Russia. Had Ian assumed that three was simply a more manageable number for me? Didn't he know that Attention Deficit Disorder aside, I could take copious notes? But no, he offered just one imperative for each letter of my ADD.

"So, what are these three imperatives?" I inquired.

"First," he continued, "stay alive. Second, secure the package. Third, get out alive."

"Secure the package?" I asked, incredulously. "Secure the package? Ian, Anna and I are going to Russia to adopt a *baby*, not to secure a package of microfilm for MI6 or perhaps letters of transit for Humphry Bogart in *Casablanca*."

Still, I was worried. After all, he and Ruthie had recently adopted in Russia. They knew firsthand it was a place just as dangerous, filled with just as much desperation and desire as Nazi-occupied Casablanca during WWII.

Anna and Ruthie were friends since kindergarten. She and Ian had put us in touch with the same Russian adoption agency they had used a few years earlier to adopt their little Russian boy. But whereas our wives had been friends for life, I had first met Ian just a few months ago. After the introduction by our wives, I found out that Ian and I had a few mutual Bostonian acquaintances. From them I got the distinct sense that Ian was former British intelligence, although no one would admit it. When I pressed her on this at home one day, Anna assured me Ian had a career as an actuary. She'd claimed he'd lost those two missing fingers at work in "some kind of industrial accident."

"What kind of industrial accident does an actuary have?" I'd asked Anna when we had been packing for our first trip to Russia one month earlier. "Did he sever two fingers from a particularly bloody paper cut? Did a thick insurance policy fall on his hand and crush two digits beyond repair? Did he suffer an incurable infection after a deadly paper clip —?"

"Oh, just some random freak accident," she interrupted, waving her hand nonchalantly as she continued packing a few dozen pairs of underwear and wool socks for our one-week trip. It was going to be cold. Beyond cold. "Kind of thing that happens all the time," she'd casually added.

Now, as I sipped cold black coffee at Ian's kitchen table, I stared into the whites of his somewhat beady bloodshot spy eyes and whispered, "I've often speculated why you don't return to England. Did you abscond with the church funds? Runoff with an MP's wife? I like to think you killed a man. It's the romantic in me."

The tiniest smile slowly paddled across Ian's craggy square British face and then sank into the ocean of his cheeks. I knew I had the bastard now. He *had* to confess to his MI6 wet work.

"I've seen *Casablanca*, David," he said, "I know that line."

By now Anna had her winter coat on and was heading toward their front door. I squeakily pushed my wooden kitchen chair back on the linoleum, stood up, and shook Ian's cold three-fingered hand. Did his hand feel as odd to him as it did to me?

"Call me if you ever need help with anything *actuarial*," he boomed much too loudly, making sure our wives hugging by the door would hear that we were just ending our perfunctory small talk. Then he leaned over to me and whispered, "remember, get out—*alive*."

Anna and I had met ten years earlier. Then, I felt young and vibrant, brimming with optimism about life's endless possibilities. We'd tried to conceive on our own naturally, then unnaturally, with ever more invasive medical intervention for years, until, half a decade later, we turned to adoption. By that time, my youth and vibrancy had yielded to wrinkles and reluctance. Still, how could I deny the woman I loved the one thing for which she yearned? She'd spent her entire career as a child therapist passionately devoted to helping other people's screwed up kids. Wouldn't it be criminal to deny her the chance to screw up her own?

Stayin' Alive

A few weeks later, planning for our second Russia trip, Anna asked, "David, do you want to go the American Medical Clinic in Moscow, or the Russian one? The American one will take an additional day." I'd previously assured her that, being of Ukrainian descent, I knew dealing with Russia—let alone adopting there—wouldn't be easy. Still, I said, I'd heard somewhere that we only had to worry about three simple things: getting in alive, getting the baby, getting out alive. The rest would be as simple as, oh, say, a Russian chess match.

During our previous, first weeklong trip to Russia, Anna knew I was already worried about the time I had taken off from running my small financial consulting company. We'd already traveled to Russia to meet the baby, Vladislav Nikolayevich Gogol, or Vladi, as we affectionately nicknamed him, at the orphanage every day for a week. Now we were back in the States, planning our second Russia trip, during which we would have to appear before the Supreme Court to beg them to give us little Vladi. But the Court appearance would be after our Russian medical exam. Well, eight medical exams. Eight different doctors in eight different medical fields. It would be so thorough, I thought, if they don't let us adopt, they'll at least say we qualify for the cosmonaut training program.

"Well here's the thing," I told Anna, "it's true that I'm worried about time and expense, but as my Ukrainian grandfather used to say, in for a kopeck, in for a ruble, and, further, I'll be damned if I'm going to go to some 1950s Soviet era clinic and have them start taking x-rays with God knows what leaky old radioactive equipment they dragged from Nikita Khrushchev's basement in 1958. Let's take the extra day and go American."

The temperature in Moscow was a slightly chilly minus 22 Fahrenheit that fateful medical morning. Our driver picked us up at the hotel in a classic Russian Lada. These cars were built like Soviet T-34 tanks in World War II. I wanted to hold the door open for Anna, and in a quick 20 or 30 minutes I'd pried the frozen 500-pound steel car door loose from its Titanic frame. Anna and I climbed in, then I sealed the hatch. The Lada slowly lumbered down the frozen tundra road, crunching snow and ice and Nazi invaders underneath the tank like tracks of its thunderous heavy tires. Anna sat in back, while I rode shotgun up front next to our tank commander, I mean, driver. He was a strong, black haired, swarthy Slavic ex-soldier (he kept his Russian army hat, which he had on the rear deck of the car peeking out the back window). As he guided the Lada toward the medical clinic, he very slowly spoke what I believe were his very first English words.

Looking sideways at me, he said, "yoooo luuuuke like Bruce Villis," in a deep resonant voice.

Now understand, I'm five feet eleven inches tall, blond, and of slight frame. In short, not quite a dead ringer for the very bald, very muscular Mister Willis. I wasn't sure how to respond to this astounding pronouncement; however, since all I'd learned to say in Russian was hello, good morning, how are you, and thank you, that's exactly what I then said, in Russian. Hello. Good morning. How are you? Thank you.

The driver looked at me again. He appeared puzzled by my sparkling Russian. His forehead and face were broad, his eyes were bottomless black-holes, and then he said, in a slow, deep, bass voice, "Yoooo luuuuke like Bruce Villis."

Just then I saw two things. Two important things. The first was an enormous poster of, you guessed it, Bruce Willis, on the side of a building, as we rounded a corner, and then, in the corner of my eye, I saw a Russian-English translation book resting on the car's console between us. I instantly realized that, while I'd learned to say only hello, good morning, how are you and thank you in Russian, our driver had learned to say in English, only, you look like Bruce Willis. (I learned later that Bruce was more popular in Russia than David Hasselhoff was in Germany).

As I contemplated renewing my gym membership and buying a head razor, the Lada slowly *crunched crunched crunched* to a stop on the frozen road. I peered through my icy window and saw the magic words, in gold lettering, "AMERICAN Medical Clinic," on the brick facade of a vast building. As I pushed, shoved, and kicked open the frozen steel Lada door, I said to the driver, mustering my finest Russian accent, "have a nice day." You see, I'd borrowed his Russian-English translation book during the ride to pick up a few more fitting phrases in Russian.

He then looked at me and said, in English, "Yoooo luuuuke like Bruce Villis." He obviously hadn't had a chance to brush up on his English during the drive.

As Anna and I waited in the clinic waiting room, I realized that they must have decided to call the place the AMERICAN Medical Clinic because they'd heard we were coming. All the other patients looked Slavic, as did the staff, administrators, and doctors. After some time, I was escorted into a small examination room. Inside the room, a very tall, lithe, beautiful woman in a white lab coat appeared. She looked like Central Casting hired her for a role as "The Beautiful Russian Doctor" for a scene in *Doctor Zhivago*. In her long slender hands, she held a thick file folder which had a label on it, with the name, *Markovich, David Mark.*

The silence was as palpable as the frozen air of an interminable Russian winter. But then, at long last, she spoke.

"Pleeze, have zeet," she said, motioning to the cold steel chair behind me. "My name is Olga-Volgavolga-skylevich. I am dock-door of winfectious dizeez."

I slumped into the icy metal chair. Here we go, I thought. Now she'll tell me to roll up my sleeve or remove my shirt, while she produces a needle the size of the Kremlin and proceeds to withdraw enough blood to fill the mighty Volga River, or perhaps just enough to fill President Putin's samovar. Was the needle even sterile? Had it just been used on the last hapless American? But then, she spoke again.

Looking at the label with my name on the thick dossier she was holding, she said, "Zo, *Markovich, David Mark*—you have infection?" For one of the only times in my life, I was speechless. I was utterly astounded.

"No, no infection," I finally replied.

Another long pause. Now here we go, I was sure, time for her to pull out God knows what old needles and blood-letting equipment. So much for the staying alive part. I could picture in my mind Ian wagging one of his three right hand fingers disapprovingly as he stood over my ice-cold body at the Russian morgue to identify the dead.

Then Doctor Olga said, "Zo, *Markovich, David Mark*—never infection?"

I wanted to jump up and say, well, I *was* in the Navy, after all. I mean, what red-blooded American boy can honestly say of himself, never infection? But of course, I couldn't say that. Anna was in the waiting room, going through hell and high water to become a mom, so I said the one thing a red-blooded American Navy vet could say under the circumstances.

Jeffrey M. Feingold

"No," I said, "never infection."

Doctor Olga then looked up from the dossier at me and exclaimed with conviction, "Next!" as she stamped my dossier with the seal of approval while I was escorted to a different examination room.

As I waited alone in the next exam room, I realized the infectious doctor likely had to get back quickly to the Bolshoi Theater, from where she'd been hired to impersonate a doctor. She was a fine actress! Then another tall lithe Slavic woman in a white lab coat appeared. It may have been another beautiful Russian actress, though I've wondered to this day if it was the same woman as the first "doctor," only now in a different wig. In either case, she also had my dossier in her hands, though perhaps inside the folder was just the Moscow phone directory. "Pleez, have zeet," she said. "I am Svetlana Stevlanovovich, dock-door of oncology. Zo," she continued, reading the name on the dossier label, "*Markovich, David Mark*—you have cancer?"

I looked down at my chest, arms, legs, and feet and—through my clothes and shoes—saw no cancer. And so, I said, "no cancer."

"Good!" she said. Then a pause ensued.

Despite my surprise at emerging from my prior exam unscathed and unbloodied, I truly thought, oh no, this is it. Now she'll instruct me to remove my shirt while stepping inside a 1950s radioactive cancer-causing x-ray machine. Or worse, ask me to remove other parts of clothing. Then what frozen steel implements from Hell would she be removing from her freezer to poke, prod and dissect me with?

After a pause, during which she looked intently through my file, perhaps trying to see if "*Markovich, David Mark*" was listed in the Moscow phone book, she said, "zo—never cancer?"

I paused and, in a flash, thought of a million biting things to say. But biting only my tongue I said the only thing possible. "No. Never cancer."

And then, concluding the exhaustive examination, she said, "next" as she stamped my file with the seal of approval.

I was thusly escorted into five more exam rooms, meeting each time some of the loveliest actresses Moscow had to offer. I don't even recall their medical specialties at this point, nearly a decade on. I think I was "examined" by specialists in feet, livers, eyes, and whatnot. But I sure do remember the last exam. After each of my first seven exams, Anna was led to the same doctor and given the exact same "examinations." But for the eighth and final exam, we were both mysteriously led together into the same exam room. After a while, a spectacled man in a white lab coat appeared, holding two separate Moscow phone directories. Apparently, Anna was listed in the Moscow phone book, too.

The man then said, "Pleez, zit down. My name is Yevgeny Yevtushenko. I am dock-door of zychology."

OK, I thought, here's where they get us. Here's where the adoption process ends. The psychologist actor will start asking us if we like to beat children, drink too much, smoke that American pot, or perhaps wear tie-dye tee shirts and listen to the Grateful Dead.

Doctor Yevgeny looked up at me, then down at the label on the dossier, and asked, "zo, *Markovich, David Mark*, you have phobia?"

I wanted to tell this man so many things. Of my fear of aging. My worries about the future. My fear that we're sullying our little planet beyond the point of no return. And most especially of my fear of having to pay a lot of actors in Russia to pretend to be doctors. Couldn't we just have skipped the eight-way medical and mailed them a check? Or left a large brown paper bag stuffed with rubles with the receptionist? But with my poor, bedraggled Anna by my side, I said the only thing possible.

"No, no phobia."

The doctor nodded his head slowly, then inquired, "Never phobia?"

After I then confirmed I had spent a lifetime free of phobias, he asked Anna the same two questions, to which she provided the same two obligatory answers.

"Good!" said the doctor, and then Anna and I were escorted back to the Lada.

Our driver was waiting, with the engine running. After sealing Anna in the rear gun turret, I again climbed into the front, sealed the hatch, and smiled at our driver, who looked me up and down and said knowingly, "yoooo luuuuke like Bruce Villis."

Securing the Package

Now that my wife and I had been officially pronounced free of cancer, bloodborne diseases, phobias, and five other conditions, the specifics of which I still don't recall, we were whisked off that very afternoon to the Supreme Court in Russia.

From Moscow, our driver and translator flew with us the five hundred miles east to the city of Kazan, where we were to be escorted to the Supreme Court of Tatarstan, the Russian province from which we were adopting. Having been at the helm of a small airplane myself, I was rather nervous as we boarded the rickety-looking puddle-jumper flown by Tartar Air. In truth, I wondered if we'd make it alive. My fears weren't unfounded: a few years later, Tartar Air was shuttered permanently after a crash in Kazan killed all aboard.

The temperature was minus twenty-two degrees Fahrenheit in Kazan as our stalwart Russian driver pulled up in front of the Supreme Court in the rental Lada. I was in the front seat of yet another heavy tank-like Soviet-era beast which our driver had rented at the airport, while Anna sat in back manning the gun turrets. After I pushed open the frozen steel Lada door with my now bruised right shoulder, I thanked the driver in Russian. He then said the only phrase in

English he'd yet learned, and which he'd previously repeated so many times to me, "yoooo luuuke like Bruce Villis."

Glancing at the Supreme Court behind me, as I used my ripping Willis-like *Die Hard* muscles to pull the frozen rear Lada door open to assist Anna, I was aghast. The Court was colossal. It appeared to be composed of two mammoth angled stone buildings which met at the front, where they connected to what must be described as the most humongous, thousand-foot-high glass penis-shaped tower in the world. I imagined bedraggled, shackled criminals cringing in fear as they were dragged forcibly into this daunting structure.

In the courtroom, Anna and I waited in the dock, seated behind a long wooden rail which separated the Judge from the damned. The Judge's heavy wooden chair, as tall as Czar's Nicholas's throne, was empty. The chair, itself seven or eight feet high, adorned with ornate carvings and red velvet inserts, sat atop a high platform several feet above the floor. Sitting in the dock, this required one to look upward quite a bit, adding even more drama to what already felt ominous. On the wall behind the throne, large portraits of Lenin and Vladimir the Great peered out at me. They looked displeased. They did not look as if they thought it was a good idea for me to be there. Vladimir Ilyanov Ulyanov, better known as Lenin, and Vladimir Sviatoslavich, better known as Vladimir the Great, glowered at me with a mendacious look which seemed to say, *"no baby for you!"*

To my right sat the Russian social worker there to represent us to the Court. To my left sat my wife. To her left sat our translator. And to his left sat an enormous bag stuffed with gifts. Gifts for the Judge, for the social worker, for the court administrator, and for the prosecutor, who was there to represent the State against these two unworthy Americans.

There was a lavishly carved wooden door between the two large portraits of the Vlads. This was the door to the Judge's personal chambers. We all rose as this door now slowly creaked open. Then, high above us, stood the Judge, who was nearly seven feet tall, wearing a thick, black, flowing velvet robe which descended in billows from his neck down to his shoes. The robe was decorated with red piping and fancy embroidery. I had to bend my neck back considerably to look up at this noble giant now towering above me as he sat on what seemed like his multistory throne. The Judge's large head was fronted by an oval face with a strong, chiseled bone structure. All in the dock now sat down.

The prosecutor stood at a podium halfway between the Judge and those seated in Court. She was a short, thin, angular woman, with a sour expression, cropped dark hair pulled back tightly, thick round heavy black glasses, an olive-drab official state uniform of some kind, and pointy black shoes. She was a dead ringer for the Russian spy in the early Bond flick, *From Russia with Love*. There she stood before me, Rosa Klebb of SPECTRE, about to tap her shoe on the floor to release the poisoned-tipped knife from the toe, just as she had to try to kill Sean Connery's James Bond in the movie. I wanted to lean over to Anna and whisper in Russian, *"Don't fuck with this one."* But, as all I'd learned to say in Russian was "hello, how are you, good afternoon, and thank you," I decided Russian was out of the question. So, I leaned over and whispered it in English.

Through our translator, seated by us, we heard the Judge speak. The Judge's voice resonated Russian words in deep, somber tones. He explained that he may not be able to let us have this baby, because too many Americans wanted Russia's precious children. And there had been incidents. In one case, he continued, an adopted child died while in America. He looked through a chunky file on his desk, then down at Anna, and explained that, although she appeared to be a lovely woman, if he let her take the baby, and if she, then, through neglect or otherwise, killed the child, well, that could "cause an international incident between our two countries." He explained that he couldn't allow himself to be responsible for such an international incident.

I was sure Anna had no intention of sparking a conflict between Russia and the United States. Not to mention that she worked in the field of child wellbeing, had spent her entire adult life helping children in need, and would sooner slit her wrists than hurt a child while starting the third and final world war. Still, it sounded like the adoption was dead in the water.

The Judge perused his file again for a few moments and then, looking down at me, noted that there was a legal technicality. He said that the file showed that I was a felon, and that Russian law prohibited him from giving Russia's precious babies to felons and other vile criminals. I was stunned. I didn't recall now having committed any major crimes. Then, regaining composure, I began to stand up to explain that there simply must be a mistake in my dossier, as I was an accountant, not an axe murderer. If they could just show me their files, I could point out where the typos were. But as I started to rise, I realized that in my flustered state I'd momentarily forgotten that the thick dossiers they were looking at would all be written in Russian, and, as previously noted, the only Russian words I knew were "hello, good morning, how are you, and thank you." Those didn't seem to be helpful in the moment. Somehow, I'd failed to learn how to say or read in Russian, "hello, good morning, how are you, I am not a vile criminal nor a felon." That lesson was somehow left out of the little bit of Rosetta Stone I'd practiced before the trip. I felt defeated as I plopped back down in my seat, sure that the Judge would deny us the baby, since my wife was a baby killer, and I was a vile axe murderer.

Then something extraordinary happened.

The prosecutor, standing with her grim, stern expression at the podium, spoke to the Judge (in Russian, which our translator translated for me and my wife). "Your Honor," she began, "I agree that the law is clear. Our precious Russian babies cannot be adopted by vile criminals. But the defendant cannot be a vile criminal, regardless of what his dossier says."

"Why is that?" the Judge inquired.

"Because, Your Highest Honor, he has a Russian visa granted for the adoption. And he would not have been granted this specific type of visa if he was a felon or other vile criminal. So, therefore, since he has this Russian visa, he cannot be a vile criminal, and His Highest Honor may, should he wish, grant him our precious Russian baby." A tiny little smile of smugness swam across Ms. Klebbs' sharp face as she congratulated herself on her brilliant deductive reasoning.

After that bit of Russian logic, the Judge said he would retire to his chambers and weigh the matter, although, he added, things didn't look good, and he doubted he would be able to give us the baby. Furthermore, he noted he was not allowed to waive the new thirty day waiting period as we'd requested.

When Anna and I began the adoption process, a little under a year earlier, Russia had a ten-day waiting law. Once the Court approved an adoption, the adoption was still considered tentative for the following ten days. This was the period during which an interested party could object, should they be so inclined. Most couples would wait in country for the ten days, then go home with their newly adopted child right after the waiting period. This was much easier than going home after Court then back to Russia ten days later. During our adoption process, though, a new federal law was enacted, stretching the ten days to thirty days. Anna and I certainly couldn't wait in county for thirty more days following our second Russia trip. We had a teenage daughter waiting for us at home. I had a business to run. And they would have had to make room for me in the nearest Russian psychiatric ward if I needed to stay an additional month. And was it really thirty days? When we'd heard about the new law, no one could even tell us if the new requirement meant thirty calendar days, thirty workdays, or thirty Russian Orthodox calendar days or some other measure.

And we were anxious to get Vladi home. He was born prematurely, was now still underweight and underdeveloped. He spent his first five months of life in a Russian hospital. At birth, part of his intestines had to be removed. After five hospital months, he went right into the orphanage, where we first met him when he was nine months old. The

Judge explained the law allowed him to waive the thirty days only if the petitioners had a letter written in Russian, by a Russian doctor writing the letter *while in Russia,* in which it was detailed that a medical emergency required waiver of the waiting period. We had submitted such a detailed letter, the Judge noted, written—in Russian—by a Russian doctor; however, the Russian doctor writing in Russian wasn't *in* Russia at the time of writing the letter in Russian. She was in America at the time of writing the letter, and that just wouldn't do. If he were to waive the waiting period under this circumstance, such a waiver also could cause an international incident between our two nations. So, to recap, the Judge said, he doubted very much he could give us the baby, and, even if he could—though he likely couldn't—he under no circumstance could waive the thirty days.

All in the Court rose as the Judge then went into his chambers. We then all shuffled out into the hallway. I knew from her visible effort to fight back tears that my wife knew she would not get to take her new baby home. We'd visited him every day in the orphanage during our first Russia trip, and most days during this second trip. She was in love. His Red Sox theme bedroom and little Sox-themed crib were waiting for him back home. But it appeared that the empty crib there would remain so. What a maddening end to a year of Russian madness. "I'm so sorry," the Russian social worker told Anna, "we did everything we could." Once again in my mind I saw Ian wagging his disapproving finger at me.

The Court administrator then told us it was time to return to the courtroom. We shuffled back in and took our seats. We all rose as the Judge then opened his chambers door, walked into the courtroom, and ascended to his throne. His face was stone. Tears were trailing down Anna's cheeks. I was angry and hurt and confounded.

Then something extraordinary happened in Russia again.

The Judge looked down at us and said, "I have made decision. You may take baby. You seem like nice family. I also waive thirty days waiting. Take baby home now. Remember, no international incidents between our two countries."

As he then looked through our files again, he must have come across some of the photos of the baby's room we'd submitted before the trip. Holding up a photo, he smiled, looked down at us, and said, "Go Sox!"

I don't know that I can find words to describe how stunned I was by the Judge's verdict. Although I don't look a bit like Bruce Willis, despite our driver's insistence to the contrary, I suspect I may have had an expression something like Bruce Willis did, in that scene in *The Sixth Sense*, when Haley Joel Osment's character, the young boy Cole, tells the psychologist played by Bruce Wills, "*I see dead people.*" To my amazement, we'd got into Russia alive. And now we'd secured the package, as Ian would say, or, in my own parlance, we'd got the baby. But would we get out—alive? Of that, I wasn't so sure.

Getting Out—*Alive*

Although the Judge waived the waiting period, we couldn't fly home with our baby the next day. We needed to complete additional steps over the next few days before we could leave with Vladi. If we could get out at all. We'd heard from Ian and Ruthie as well as from credible sources that some Americans with their newly adopted children had recently been stopped by the FSB at airports. The FSB was the successor to the Soviet Union's KGB, and there were FSB agents now stationed at airports across Russia. There was great resentment for westerners emptying Russia of her precious babies. And more Americans than any other westerners were adopting there. Even though there were over seven hundred thousand children in orphanages across Russia, that didn't mean unworthy Americans should be taking any of them home.

Before we could take Vladi to the airport, there was more red tape. Although the Judge had waived the thirty days wait, we needed to secure the baby's exit visa and his Russian passport, and other paperwork before we could finally fly home together with Vladi.

Early that evening, as Anna slept in our hotel room, the landline hotel phone rang. While Anna slept fitfully, I had been watching television. A program about the opera house in Sydney, Australia. It was in Russian, of course, so I couldn't understand the narration, except for the parts when the narrator said things in Russian such as hello, good morning, how are you, thank you, I am not a vile criminal. When the hotel room phone rang, I picked it up quickly before Anna stirred.

"This is Ekaterina," the stern voice on the telephone said. "I am Prosecutor from Supreme Court."

"Oh," I replied, instantly fearful of bad news. My heart skipped a beat. "Ekaterina, you speak … English?"

"Da," she said. "Such a crude, vile language! Zo, you wish keep baby?"
"Well, yes, Anna and I wish that very much."

"Da," she said, "You must spell baby name."

I began to spell Vladi's name slowly. "V.L.A.D.I.S.L.A.V." Then I began on his middle name, but as I tried to spell Nikolayevich, I realized something important: I didn't know how to spell Nikolayevich. I started, "N.I.K.O.L." then realized something else: surely the Russian Prosecutor must know how to spell such a venerable Russian name?

"Ms. Prosecutor, don't *you* know how to spell it?"

"Da. Zo you keep baby name?"

After another minute of this back-and-forth Russian Round Robin, the lights in the dark Kremlin recesses of my brain finally flicked on. I realized what this conversation really was. She was asking if Anna and I would keep the baby's birth names, Vladislav Nikolayevich (we would of course drop the surname, Gogol), or if we would instead change his names. I already knew that Anna and I wanted little Vladi to have a more American first name at least, something to give him a fighting chance at the playground. But what name?

"Ms. Esteemed Prosecutor," I said, "Anna and I thought we'd get to choose the baby's name after we got him home."

"*Nyet!*" she exclaimed. "I must go to Ministry of Administration tomorrow morning to deliver paperwork in triplicate. Papers will take me all night. I must have baby name now for paperwork."

"Anna is sleeping," I noted. "Can I discuss this with her and then call you back in an hour or two?"

"You have fifteen minutes," she declared. I wondered if she was freshening up the poison on her poison-tipped stiletto shoe in the event we failed when the time was up. I was also regretting letting our translator in on that little Rosa Klebb joke of mine that day in Court.

"I understand," I said. "I'll wake up Anna now."

"I will call you back. You now have—*precisely fourteen minutes eight seconds.*"

Click.

I quietly shuffled to the bedside and began gently stroking Anna's smooth black hair. "Anna, Anna, my gentle wife, wake up, we have to choose a name for little Vladi." I looked at the blue face of the Omega Speedmaster on my wrist to see what little time we had left was speeding away. Poor gentle Anna was exhausted.

"I'm going to *punch you out* if you don't let me sleep, for God's sake" she mumbled, half-awake.

"Punch. That' a great name. But not exactly the name I was thinking of," I told her.

After she fully awoke, I filled her in on the situation. I looked at my wristwatch and said nervously, "we have exactly nine minutes and eight seconds left."

By then it was coal black outside. Although the curtains were open, the brightest thing in the hotel room was the television screen. We both gazed into the TV intently for a solid two minutes, reducing our precious remaining baby naming-for-life time to less than seven minutes. The television screen showed a stunning view of the Sydney Opera House. Its sunlit snow-white interlocking shells reflected in the surrounding blue ocean, the slowly undulating water transforming the reflected shells into billowing sails waiving in the warm Australian breeze. It was breathtaking.

"Sydney?" I said to Anna.

"Yes," she said, "Sydney."

At precisely fifteen minutes and zero seconds after the Prosecutor's first call, the hotel phone rang again.

"Sydney," I said into the phone receiver. "The baby's name is Sydney."

"Kidney?" the Prosecutor said, "How you spell?"

I wondered—would we *ever* get the hell out of here?

A few days later, all the red tape sealed, our driver picked us up at the hotel to drive us to the airport. At last, we were going home! Syd was already with us. Our driver drove us to the orphanage to get him the day before. He'd spent the night in the hotel room with us.

As I opened the heavy steel Lada door to help Anna, who was carrying little Syd, swaddled in many blankets, into the back seat, I was stunned to see the Prosecutor already sitting bolt upright in the back. This could be bad, I thought, looking down at her shoes. I got into the front seat, sealed the Lada hatch, then looked back at the Prosecutor.

"Ms. Prosecutor," I said, "I didn't expect to see you here." I feared the worst.

"Da," she said. "But even with his Highest Honor's approval, some Americans have not left country with babies. I make sure you go home. Nice family."

I was astounded. "I don't know what to say, Ekaterina. We are forever in your debt."

"I may have knife in shoe," she said, "but I do not have stone in heart." A tiny little smile of sweetness swam across her now softened face as she congratulated herself on her sparkling poetic wit.

At the airport, heavily armed burly FSB agents in olive-drab uniforms were everywhere. Anna, Syd and I walked alongside Ekaterina toward the security checkpoint we had to clear first to then walk to our gate. As we got close to the checkpoint, my blood boiled. Then I saw one of the agents lean over to another and, looking directly at Ekaterina, whisper in Russian, *"don't fuck with this one."* I had picked up, you see, a few more fitting Russian phrases during our stay.

And that is how, at the age of one, Vladislav Nikolayevich Gogol of Russia became the American, Sydney Mark Markovich, or Syd for short. When he was two, Anna and I took Syd to his first Boston Red Sox game. He never took his eye off the ball. And neither had we.

Epilogue

Sadly, though, our marriage didn't hold forever and, a few years after adopting, Anna and I divorced. But though a divorce marks the death of a dream, I've come to understand it's not the end of the journey. Anna and I still see each other every other day, as we're amicably co-parenting Syd.

I guess the heaviness of aging and parenting and perhaps of just *being* eventually weighed us down until it overtook us. Still, over time, Anna and I reached some new understanding of each other, and, perhaps, of ourselves. At least, I like to think so. And we always have our Syd, as I pointed out to Anna one day.

"Not only that," I said to her that sunny spring afternoon, as we waited for Syd's school bus in the front yard of her yellow New England farmhouse, standing under cheerful cherry blossoms blushing as pink as the cheeks of newborn babes, "we'll always have Moscow."

My now ex-wife looked at me. The tiniest smile slowly paddled across her beautiful soft face and then sank into the ocean of her cheeks. "I've seen *Casablanca*, David," she said, "I know that line." And then, "do you have regrets?"

I looked down at my chest, arms, legs, and feet and -through my clothes and shoes - saw no regrets. And so, I said, "no, never. Never regrets."

Just then a bright yellow school bus came to a halt at the end of the driveway. The door squeaked open, and out barreled Sydney Mark Markovich, as strong as a Russian bull and as American as apple pie.

I leaned into Anna and whispered, *"don't fuck with this one."*

●

Avalanche

I wondered, would I die of dehydration or hypothermia? Then the thought occurred to me: I was buried in an avalanche, high up in the Alps. So, it wouldn't be dehydration. I had only to stick out my tongue to access an endless amount of snowy hydration. It would be the cold that would take me. Not a pleasant way to go, I thought. But just then, I heard it: the unmistakable sound of giant paws digging frantically through the snow. I was saved! My trusty Saint Bernard, Wenny, was rescuing me. After some more frantic digging, the blankets I was crouched under came off. I was sitting on the cold kitchen floor playing her favorite game: Alpine Rescue. For centuries, monks in the St. Bernard Pass, a treacherous route through the Italian and Swiss Alps, eight thousand feet above sea level, relied on Saint Bernards to save thousands of hapless travelers. And now, just a few feet above kitchen floor level, my wonderful Saint saved me during our daily game. Once the "snow" blankets were removed, she hurled herself—all one hundred forty pounds—on my lap and began licking my face. It's then I thought she must be made of one hundred thirty pounds of muscle and determination and ten pounds of tongue. How I adored her.

This was a bit after our family's dog adventures began. One year earlier, when my daughter was about six years old, I wanted to get her first dog. I was thinking a beagle, as that was my childhood dog, and what a wonderful dog she was (even though she betrayed me by refusing to eat my mother's hard-as-nails quick-boiled Brussels sprout when I surreptitiously slipped them to her under the kitchen table at supper. Still, she was otherwise a loyal companion for a lonely, quirky child).

And so, I began thinking of getting a beagle for my only child. But my wife convinced me that a bigger dog would be best, one that our daughter could be more physically active with. I searched around and found a candidate at a local shelter. His name was Andy. He was half golden Labrador, half Greyhound. He was a street stray when he was found and brought to the shelter two weeks earlier. The shelter staff gave him the name Andy, which seemed an odd dog name to me, at first, and yet, as soon as my wife, daughter and I met him at the shelter, we thought that somehow Andy was the only name possible. His age was indeterminate, but the shelter's vet thought he was likely six to eight years old. He was tan, with a long nose, a lean face shaped like a Greyhound, and with the sweet floppy ears of a Labrador. He was both handsome and goofy looking at the same time. His brown eyes were large and soulful. And, while he didn't have a lot of teeth left, he seemed somehow as lighthearted, kind, and wise as Sheriff Andy Taylor in "The Andy Griffith Show." So, we brought him home one Saturday morning. Considering that we lived in an old farmhouse in a quiet suburb, now with wise old Andy, I practically expected Opie, Barney and Aunt Bee to come strolling up to the front door with an apple pie any minute as we hung around the house that weekend.

My daughter's bedroom was so small that she had a day bed, with a pull-out trundle on wheels underneath. That weekend, each night, I'd pull out the trundle, which had its own guest mattress, and my daughter would sleep on the day bed while Andy slept beside her on the trundle bed. So sweet. It was a peaceful weekend with our little now extended family. We all thought Andy was the bomb. And then first thing Monday morning, the little bastard ran away. I was preparing to drive my daughter to school and to take Andy to work with me. My hands were full, with his bowls, blankets, and toys, and as I cracked open the door he slipped out in a flash. That's when the Greyhound kicked in. He shot down the street like an arrow, as straight and as fast. I told my daughter to wait at the door then dashed off after Andy. I still had his bowls and blankets in my hands. After a few minutes, with him getting further from me by the moment, he began to run into the backyards of neighbors, as I began to realize I'd never catch him. Panic streaked through my mind. What would I tell my daughter? How could I tell her I'd just lost her first dog? At this point, Andy was running in and out of view many houses away. In exasperation and exhaustion, I dropped to my knees and began calling for him as I furiously waived his blanket overhead. He saw the blanket and immediately ran straight toward me. Apparently, the waiving blanket was his signal that the game was now to catch me. I dropped his things and picked him up. All sixty-five lanky, long-legged pounds. I carried him home, both relieved and ripping mad.

Over the next year, Andy settled in nicely. There were many morning walks to school with the three of us: Andy, my daughter and me. But as the year dragged on, his eyes seemed a little more soulful, he somehow lost more teeth, and I wondered if he needed both dentures and canine companionship during the long school and workdays.

Since dentures weren't an option, I went to work on the companionship. Turns out that my daughter's school crossing guard often brought her son's Saint Bernard with her in the morning. She told me about the farm where her Saint was from, and in time I planned to get a Saint Bernard puppy.

Wenny was just twelve weeks old and twelve pounds when she came home. She liked me to carry her on one of my shoulders around the house. Six months later, at eighty-five pounds, she still wanted to be carried. Every time we played Alpine Rescue, after she dug me out of the "snow," she'd walk past me, stop, then start to back up towards me to deposit her rather oversized bottom on one of my shoulders. I obliged her as long as I could, until her girth and weight became just too much. I think it helped my chiropractor to send his kids to college. But by the time Wenny reached one hundred pounds—soon to be one hundred forty—shoulder rides were out of the question.

My wife and daughter and I were sure Wenny still saw herself as that little dainty pup she was when we first brought her home. Her favorite treat was blueberries. But they'd have to be small, and she'd eat just one at a time. But when she was about nine or ten months old, her lips seemingly drooped overnight. She got jowls. Lots of them. I'd take a little blueberry, place it in the folds of her mouth, and she'd proceed to roll and roll and roll it around. About five minutes later, *plop*! The berry popped out of her mouth onto the floor. I'd stick it in again and she'd start all over. Eventually she'd swallow the berry. You could leave a pint of fresh blueberries on the kitchen counter and not worry that she'd eat them all because it would have taken her about a decade.

Andy and Wenny got on just dandy. But in a few years, poor old Andy died. Not long after, Maggie the Basset Hound puppy came into our lives. She was all ears. They were so long that when she was a pup her ears would drag along the floor as she tore through the house. She often tripped on them. She and Wenny adored each other. She was crazy and sweet and as soft as a velveteen rabbit. She lived with us for several years after Wenny passed.

This isn't that type of dog story, though. You know the kind: about my old dog, Blue, who when he died, I didn't know what to do, etc., etc.. No, this is a love letter to dogs. But of course, eventually all our furry friends do pass. When Wenny died, a year after getting bone cancer, my wife said it was the first time she'd seen me cry in our decade together. She was right. I'd learned long ago how to compartmentalize. And yet, the hatch to the compartment where my tears had been bottled and stored did open that day of Wenny's death.

A few years later, Maggie the Bassett died, a year after her first stroke. I found myself sitting next to her on the vet exam room floor. Just me and my old hound dog. After the deed was done, sitting by her still, warm body, I cried. A lot. The door to that compartment was now flung open wide. I cried for her year of struggle, and because I knew how much I would miss her tomorrow and for many tomorrows. I cried because I couldn't save her, as I couldn't save Wenny. I think I cried because I couldn't save anyone. Not my Dad, who'd died of cancer a year before my daughter was born. Not my broken marriage. Not my Nana, who'd died when I was just a scrawny little boy with a pocket full of poems and a head full of fantasies.

Nana died in front of me, in the very doctor's office in which, just a few years earlier, I'd run to the bathroom to get a feminine napkin to save her from the terrible embarrassment of having her chocolate ice cream cone drip onto her lovely blue and white polka dot dress. I had no idea what a feminine napkin was. I thought it was just a really, really well constructed napkin, and I would be her savior in bringing one to her. But it was the wrong napkin, and I didn't save her from her dripping ice cream. And now as she lay dying, flat upon the cold waiting room floor, no one could save her from something much more terrible than a messy dress. The doctor and nurse dragged her into his office and shut the door. I never saw her again. It was my first exposure to the shock of the suddenness of death. I ran to find the nearest payphone to call my parents. But she was already gone. I didn't cry, I suppose from the shock. I learned to compartmentalize.

Now, though, a lifetime later, next to Maggie the Bassett, I finally cried for Nana. There was quite an avalanche of tears with no Saint Bernard to dig me out. I hadn't saved Maggie, Wenny, Andy, my Dad, so many dead aunts, uncles, friends, pets, marriages, and dreams.

And so, I cried now for them all, and for myself. But then, after a while, I just stopped crying. I closed the hatch and sealed it again. I smiled a little, like Paul Newman at the end of *Cool Hand Luke,* when he's surrounded by guards after his prison break, and he realizes there's no exit. Looking up to the heavens, he asks if God is up there. When there's no answer, he says, alright, guess that's the way you're gonna' play it, huh? I felt that way. So, I told Maggie it was time for me to go.

●

I was born, if I may humbly note, for greatness. Specifically, literary greatness. While I'll never pen a terrific two-ton tome like *Ulysses*, James Joyce and I have something great in common. Not height, nor looks, nor vision, nor the ability to play the Irish drum; I'm taller, after all, better looking if I may immodestly suggest, with far sharper eyesight, and a fair bit of a better bodhran player. The greatness we share is this: we were both censored. Our books burned. Joyce's sprawling *Ulysses* and my humble poetry made us both brothers in banishment. In my case, though, the banishment was from a little bit of ancient tech in the olden days that we used to call, "radio." Radio stations still used recording tape back in the Stone Age when I attended college. My poems weren't so much burned as erased.

I was sitting in a tiny spartan room just outside the recording studio of the local public radio station near my school, waiting my turn. The station had invited listeners to record their poems, which were later to be aired all day, dawn to dusk, on June 16 – Bloomsday, as is now celebrated around the world—the day depicted in Joyce's *Ulysses*. As I waited, I heard something strange. A disembodied voice emanating from the speaker over my head whispered,

"When you touch me,
  Every fiber of my being recoils,
  In mortal *terror*,"

The incorporeal voice continued:

"Every red blood corpuscle *implodes*,
  Every strand of DNA *unwinds*,
   Every atom *atomizes*.
    Your touch is my cells in the blackness,
    shrieking."

As I was alone in the waiting room, I stood up and peered into the recording booth. A lithe young woman stood at the microphone, her

DNA and atoms now screaming poetry into the MIC. A portrait in black: black jeans, tee shirt, Army boots. Anthracite hair. Eyes black as the dark side of the moon. Cold. Remote. Instantly, I was in love.

Her reading finished, she opened the door between the recording studio and waiting room and boot-shuffled in. She gazed at me first with haughtiness, then diffidence. So alluring! I wanted to ask her out for coffee—black coffee—but feared her atoms might shriek. Or was it her DNA? In either case, there I sat, gingerly hirsute, tan chinos, crisp white shirt, a blond-haired, blue-eyed poet about to read the poor puff poem I'd penned for this occasion. I clasped the papers in my right hand, which I turned over so that this woman, this genius, this Sylvia Plath, or Edna St. Vincent Millay, or perhaps Avril Lavigne-in-the-making, wouldn't see what drivel I had written.

Her eyes stabbed mine.

"What do you want from me?"

The first words of our budding romance.

"Just your name."

"My name?" she asked, staring at me with eyes which instantly communicated that she might, depending on her whim, love me forever, or cut my heart out to fashion an avant-garde red lampshade for her art class.

"My name is for my friends."

"I'd like to be your friend," I suggested.

"Why?"

"Because I want to know your name. Do you want to have coffee?"

"Coffee? What is this, 1930? Meet me at The Rat at ten tonight and I'll buy you a beer. Then you'll learn my name."

The station producer, in the hallway, stuck his head in the waiting room to inform me my time was at hand.

"Goodbye, Sylvia," I said to the woman in black as I opened the recording booth door.

"Goodbye, Redford," she instantly retorted.

When the rectangular red light in the booth flashed RECORDING—RECORDING—RECORDING, I read my poem, "Homage to Rod McKuen." Rod was one of the best-selling poets in the U.S. in the 1960's and 70's. His book, *Listen to the Warm*, made me want to throw up in the way that hearing a song by Henry John Deutschendorf, Jr. —better known as John Denver—did. "Rocky Mountain High" always made me feel so terribly low.

Homage to Rod McKuen

By

Jeffrey M. Feingold

I think people who run over creatures,
Should be tortured with needles or leaches,
For me it seems indubitable
That God fashioned every marsupial,
Mammal, plant, and vegetable,
Both those edible and inedible.

So, the next time you hop in your automobile,
Make sure it is only the tires that squeal,
Or else you'll be sentenced with no hope for repeal,
To needles, and leeches,
Perhaps even an eel.

If you're reading this essay, fear not, dear reader. This was the last poem I ever wrote. In that sense, I did achieve greatness and saved the world. After the recording, I went to the school library and, my upcoming date with the unnamed queen of goth poetry in mind, read every poem about death I could find. That night, I ambled over to The Rathskeller, or Rat as we called it, the pub in the student union building, just before ten o'clock. I ordered a beer at the bar. The bartender slid the frosty bottle to my stool while slowly waving a little white envelope in his other hand.

"The beer is free," he said.

"Why?"

"She paid, and she left this for you," he said, waving the envelope while chortling.

"Who?"

"The black lady." I looked around the room.

"Which black lady?"

"No, I mean the lady, in black."

"The sacred pint alone can unbind the tongue," I told the bartender, sipping the beer while quoting from *Ulysses*.

"Redford, you seem nice," the note said. "Don't get me wrong, it's just that nice isn't my thing. I'm not saying you're not pretty. I'm just saying you're the light; I'm the dark. Be well, Goth Girl." Who was this mystery woman? This woman in black? This black hole?

The next day was June 16. I planted myself in front of the transistor radio in my dorm room and did not move from dawn to dusk. Around dinnertime, I heard her. At first a whisper, then louder, growing ever louder into a scream. It was her alright, Goth Girl, imploding and unwinding and atomizing and shrieking. The same disembodied voice shooting from the speaker into my brain, from the cortex all the way down to the basest primitive impulses in my medulla oblongata.

It was my turn next. I was bursting with excitement, about to hear my own poem on the radio. Radio, of all things. What a hoot! But instead of hearing my deep, manly, rather attractive baritone, if I may say, I heard some mousy guy squeaking out his poem.

The Pussycat
By
Morton Feary Cuthbert, III

The pussycat is a noble critter
Who'll only poop in clean cat litter,
Who'll only eat from clean bright dishes
The freshest Grade A tuna fishes;
Yes, the pussycat has beaten the puppy,
To become the first domesticated yuppy.

And then the program was over. Where was my recording? My Big Moment? Could I have missed it? Did I nod off during the day long deluge of poems, from ditties to diatribes? No, I hadn't snoozed. Hadn't taken so much as even a bathroom break. How did my poem disappear into a black hole?

The next day, I called the radio station and asked to speak to the station manager.

"We were afraid your poem could have offended someone," he said.

"Who?" I said, "marsupial worshipers?"

"No," he said, "Rod McKuen."

"But it was a parody," I said, "meant to be humorous."

"Not to Rod McKuen."

"You didn't censor the girl who was imploding and unwinding and atomizing and shrieking?"

"Well, she didn't offend Rod McKuen."

And just like that, James Joyce and I become brothers in banishment. As for Goth Girl, I never did get her name. But I like to imagine she's still out there in the world, somewhere. Waiting to return. Someday we'll meet again. Goth Girl. She's the poet the world deserves, to paraphrase the Dark Knight, but not the one it needs right now.

●

The Buzz Bomb

The Nazis never did catch me. I was an explosives expert, and I was just too good for them. I could blast my way out of any situation, no matter how dire. I was seven or eight years old, growing up in the pretend war-torn streets of inner-city Boston. My friends and I were always playing war games. We were children of the Greatest Generation, after all, living out our foolish fantasies in the shadow of real heroes who had saved the world.

Bobby was our communications expert. He had two Campbell's Soup cans, labels removed, wire strung between the bright shiny silver canisters, and then from one can another wire running to a small wooden box to which the rotary dial from a telephone had been affixed. Using this brilliant homemade piece of kit, he could "radio" headquarters anytime, anywhere. It had no batteries, of course, but it never failed him. Still, if our little band of brothers found ourselves trapped, with Nazi tanks closing in on all sides—no time to wait for the reinforcements Bobby had called for—everyone knew they could count on me to blast our way out in the nick of time.

No matter how bad things got, we'd all be home in time for American Chop Suey and, at least in my case, Brussels sprout boiled so briefly they were as hard as the "Superballs" we bounced on the city sidewalks. Bobby, Johnny, Danny, Jimmy—why did all my friends' names end in y back then?—they all knew I had their backs. I carried a pillowcase full of demolition stuff, just like David Niven in *The Guns of Navarone*, which my Dad and I watched every time it aired on television.

In my bag of tricks, I had firecrackers, of course, but also cherry bombs (you could lose a finger if not careful when one of those went off), M-80s (you could lose a hand), Roman Candles (you could lose an eye and quite possibly two), and more. You name it, I had it. And it was all legal back then, in the old days. Our patrol squad would get on our ten-speed bikes Saturday mornings and go off to fight the good fight.

The war never seemed to end back then, it dragged on, year after bloody year, and just as strangely, was only fought on Saturdays. "Just be home by supper," my mom would holler through the kitchen door at breakfast, as I dashed down our steps, a half-eaten bagel dangling from my war-weary lips. Then I'd mount my orange ten speed Huffy bicycle to speed off to the frontlines. "And don't lose any fingers," she'd holler as I sped away. That was it. Helicopter parenting hadn't been invented yet. Just be home for supper and you damn well better bring all your digits with you. If we must bring you to the hospital, you'll be sorry! Other than that, no worries. What happened at the front stayed at the front.

And I always did come home, in time for supper, and with all digits accounted for. Until it happened one day. It was an accident, of course. In my bag of tricks, among the sundry explosives, I had a very special device called a "buzz bomb." It was a long tube, longer than your middle finger, densely packed with gunpowder. On one end of the tube was a small propeller. On the other end, two long fuses. I'd twist the two fuses together into one, place the bomb on a flat surface such as a picnic table, light the end of the fuses with a match, and then the bomb would shoot straight up into the air, the propeller whirling furiously, as a wide, dense shower of yellow sparks descended from the tube's tail, showering everything underneath it in a glittering display.

The bomb didn't really buzz at all; it emitted more of a hissing sound. But I confess I appreciated the alliterative "buzz bomb" and was glad it hadn't been named the "hissy bomb."

On this one Saturday, we'd all ridden our ten speeds to a nearby park. The patrol stood fifty yards away from me, in a wooded area, next to a clump of big oak trees, while I placed a buzz bomb on a picnic table. I twisted the two fuses together. I then struck a match and lit the end of the fuses.

That's when disaster struck.

Only one of the two fuses caught. A few seconds later the fuse burned down and ignited the gunpowder. Only, instead of shooting straight up into the air and emitting a shower of relatively harmless sparks, the buzz bomb steaked straight ahead as fast as a missile. It headed straight to the clump of oaks where my friends stood.

Upon impact with one of the trees, the bomb exploded with a tremendous thunderclap. Thick black smoke enshrouded the patrol. I ran as fast as the wind to them. Bobby was shaking his head. I think he couldn't hear very much due to the deafening explosion. "Hold up your hands," I said.

He shook his head side to side, "What? What did you say?"

"Hold up your hands," I yelled so loudly that the other guys covered their ears. Bobby finally heard me, and he held up both hands. I counted ten digits. "Thank God for that!" I said.

"Well," Bobby said, "Reckon we better clear out. That little mishap of yours just gave away our position. In minutes, this place will be swarming with Nazis."

We headed over to the picnic table to get our bikes. The guys asked what went wrong with the buzz bomb. I told them what happened with the fuses.

"I'm never using a buzz bomb again. From now on, we're playing it safe. I'll only use these," I said, as I took a new kind of cylinder from the explosives bag, and held it up for the group to see.

"That looks pretty harmless," Johnny said.

Danny didn't read very well, so we'd made him our Morse Code officer. Looking at the explosive cylinder I was holding up, and trying to read the text on the cylinder, he said, "What does that mean" and then he sounded out the letters one at a time— "W-I-D-O-W... M-A-K-E-R"?

After a brief pause, Jimmy said, "It means we ain't out the woods yet, men."

Then we all rode home. My mom's American Chop Suey never tasted more comforting. Though I still pocketed the inedible Brussels sprout when she wasn't looking. I wondered if I could drill out a hole in the sprout, put in a little gunpowder, then a fuse. Brussel Bombs!

"Son," my Dad said at dinner, "I want to ask you something important—where did your pillowcase go?"

"I lost it in the war, Dad" I said.

He and my mother looked at each other, shook their heads, and returned to eating. All was well on the home front.

●

The LTD

Shortly before defeating the Nazis and winning WWII, I swore off explosives. I was always dragging around a pillowcase full of firecrackers, Cherry Bombs, Roman Candles, Buzz Bombs, and whatnot. But after a wayward Buzz Bomb hit an oak tree by my little patrol squad of fellow seven-or eight-year-old freedom fighters, I told the patrol it was time for a change.

"Shoot, so no more bombs?" Billy asked.

"That's right," I said, "it's time to put away childish things. It's time for—tanks."

We were standing on Wentworth Terrace, our little neighborhood street in Boston, standing under the blazing summer sun, and staring together at something so beautiful it nearly brought a tear to my flinty old eye. It was my father's brand-new Ford LTD sedan. It was the secret weapon to end the war once and for all. The Nazis had nothing like it. It was black, stealthy, and shinier than the smoothest obsidian ever seen on earth. The gleaming black hood, baking under the summer sun, was hot enough to fry the two eggs over easy with kippers and onions my mom made for my Dad every Sunday morning. And the LTD had rich red Corinthian leather-like vinyl seats, with a slick matching red pinstripe running along both sides from bumper to bumper. It was a tank with class. And it seemed to me and my scrawny compatriots to be at least one thousand yards long. If the entire U.S. military wouldn't fit in it, at least Patton's 3rd U.S. Army would.

It was my Dad's pride and joy. The Saturday he brought it home, friends and family came from near and far just to marvel at it. As they gave it long, loving looks, my grandfather patted my Dad on his back and said, "you have done well, son." My Dad beamed. And now it was ours—the patrol squad's—new secret war weapon.

"LTD stands for Large Tank Destroyer," I explained to the squad. At least that's what I thought it meant. "Here's the plan, men," I said. "See that brick building at the end of the street," I said, as we all looked over at our elementary school. "Well, that's the Nazi's main fuel depot. If we destroy that, the war will be won."

"That's impossible," Johnny said grimly, "just look at the depot. It's heavily mortified."

We all stared at the Emily A. Fifield School, studying it with the kind of military precision made possible by years of public school elementary education. Of course, we all went to school there five days a week, so we already knew the layout like the back of our hands. Still, we stood staring at the big brick building with its high black iron rod fence around the perimeter.

"You're right," Danny declared, "it's got way too many mortifications."

"Look," Chucky said, unfolding the paper he'd taken out of his jeans pocket, "according to this map, there's a weak point in the mortifications, right *here*." He stabbed his stubby right index finger directly on the front door of the building shown on the paper IHOP placemat.

"Wait a second, "Bobby cried, that's not a Nazi map. It's from the International House of Pancakes!"

The rest of us looked at Bobby with dismay, as if he didn't know what a map was.

"Everyone loves pancakes," I said, "even Nazis—so it *must* be their map."

There was a slight pause, then they all nodded in agreement with my sterling logic. We were ready to launch our attack on the fuel depot.

By then, all the grownups had ambled over to my folks' house to do grownup things. I instructed the patrol squad to climb into the LTD. Four or five of the guys clambered into the backseat, while a couple got in front, with me at the wheel. I wondered, is this what heaven will be like? Would it smell like this? Like a new Ford LTD? The LTD was surely as big as heaven. So big, my feet couldn't reach the floor or the pedals.

Then something terrible happened.

Back then, in the old days, people didn't worry about silly little things, like safety. Air bags hadn't been invented. Seat belts were just being introduced and most people didn't bother with them. Cars were for having fun, after all, not for party-poopers worried about safety. One safety feature now standard—the brake shift interlock—hadn't been invented yet. This lock prevents a car from being shifted when the key is not in the ignition. Because the lock didn't exist then, I was able to give the transmission shifter on the steering column a gentle tug. I heard a soft "clunk" as the car shifted into neutral.

It just so happens that Wentworth Terrace was built at a slight incline, with the school at the bottom. Our secret weapon was near the top of the street, parked on the sidewalk, with the front of the car facing the school. Only now it wasn't parked at all because I'd shifted it. The LTD began rolling. At first, almost imperceptibly. But rolling it was. Now not so imperceptibly, but rather a bit faster and inexorably toward the Nazi fuel depot and our certain doom. I tried reaching the pedals, but my legs were too short. Not that I knew which pedal was the brake, anyway. I knew it was down there, so close but so far. I was locked in a desperate struggle for survival. Not that I was worried about the Nazis now. No, in my panic, I feared Dad would ground me until I was an old man, maybe age thirty.

"I, I don't know what to do, guys," I stammered. "I can't control her," I said, as I heard a car door open behind me. Then a thud as one of the boys rolled out onto the street. Then another thud, thud, thud, thud. Then I was alone. It seemed fitting, I thought, facing my fiery fate as the tank steamrolled on toward the fuel depot. To die a hero. The boy who won the war and saved the world. It was—my destiny.

Then I heard one last thud, as I jumped out the driver's door and rolled away. In a flash I'd decided I would live to fight the war another day—most likely the next Saturday.

When I was done rolling, I shot bolt upright just in time to watch the LTD smash into the iron gate surrounding the Nazi fuel depot. Her five thousand pounds of steel and U.S. ingenuity and grit smashed right through the iron gate and into the side of the brick building. The rest of the patrol ran over to me, and we all stood and stared, dumbfounded. Little dancing yellow and orange flames licked the shiny black hood. Then the LTD exploded. The hood shot up into the air. I started shaking. Moms were running into the street. My mom ran all the way down from our house to get me.

Back at home, I was crying in my bedroom. Mom came in, sat on the floor next to me, and hugged me. She could see I was a wreck. When my Dad came home after work, she told him to leave me be for tonight, that I was already punishing myself enough. The next morning, my Dad came into my bedroom and sat on the bed beside me.

"You know, son," he said, "I really loved that car."

I was about to tell him I loved it, too, and to start balling again. But then he took my hand in his and said, "son, I have a secret weapon even better than the LTD. Better than anything in the whole war. And the Nazis don't have it. It's called *insurance*."

Later that week, my Dad drove home from work one day in the most beautiful thing I'd ever seen: a gleaming, sparkling brand new 1966 Ford Thunderbird. As I walked around the car, hand-in-hand with my Dad, I thought, oh, those Nazis are in for it now!

●

My Left Foot

"My God, you've actually done it," my wife, Anna, exclaimed as she buried the heavy black handset to our home telephone in her fuzzy pink pullover cable knit sweater so that the caller wouldn't hear her.

"It's *them!*" she added.

She looked dazed.

"That's fantastic!" I blurted out. "I can't believe it! It's really them?" I thought for a moment, then inquired, "them *who*?"

"PBS Television," she explained, keeping the handset buried. "A producer from PBS. She wants to speak to you."

I, too, was dazed, the proverbial deer in the headlights. This was it, after all. My Big Break. My Moment. Stardom was staring me in the face. And like the deer in those headlights, I wouldn't blink. The world was now my oyster. And it was about to be shucked.

I had always known this day was inevitable. As surely as the sun rises each morning, as surely as the earth turns each day, as surely as you can always rely on a succulent black pastrami sandwich, with a juicy dill pickle, from Howie the butcher at Howie's Deli on Morton Avenue in Boston, I always knew that fate, however fickle, would find fame and fortune for me.

I had known this since high school, when I felt it in my bones during the standing ovation, the thunderous applause, the electric pulse surging through my body as I bowed after mesmerizing my audience by playing an ADHD-stricken Romeo. The first ever production, I suspect, of *Romeo and Juliet* in which poor Romeo had an undiagnosed neurological condition.

"Well hot damn, that's a new one on me," Mr. Simons, my high school drama teacher, declared. "ADHD. What the heck, Simons says, let's give it a whirl!"

It was very likely the first *Romeo and Juliet* in which Romeo kept forgetting Juliet's name—as well as directions to her house. It was novel. It was daring. And just like me, it was undiagnosed. And it brought the house down. As fair, freckled Molly Finkleblatt—my first ever real-life crush—bowed to the audience, the whistles and clapping went on for many minutes. Too many minutes. It probably would have continued for hours, had not the high school custodian eventually asked my parents and the Finkleblatts to please stop clapping and sit down before they would all be expelled.

After my glory days of high school theater, I put the arts behind me and went into the Navy, then college, then business. Life took over. Marriages, mortgages, middle-age. In short, grownup type stuff. But twenty or so years later, my artistic soul was in desperate need. So, I turned back to acting.

I'd sent PBS my acting resume a month before the call, in response to their posting on an audition website. They were in search of actors for a special about Darwin. Would I be cast as the balding, mutton-chopped, pensive Darwin, I wondered, as my wife handed me the phone. Perhaps instead I'd be the terrifically handsome Alexander von Humboldt, the German naturalist and romantic philosopher who heavily influenced many of the greatest luminaries of his generation and the next, including Darwin, Whitman, Thoreau, and Emerson. Which would I be?

"We loved your resume," the woman on the phone said.

"Thanks so much," I burbled, "I've been waiting for a call like this. Which part is it for?"

"It's for Maggie," she explained.

Maggie was my wife's Basset Hound.

"There's a scene in the show when we will have a few dozen dogs, different breeds, and we'd love to have Maggie, for a Basset Hound in the mix. We're going to use the wide variety of breeds to demonstrate natural selection and biodiversity."

"Oh," I said, deflated.

"It pays really well," she replied. "And we can use your Saint Bernard, too."

"I'll have to consult with my wife," I said. "It's her Basset Hound."

Actors usually include all sorts of personal details and minutiae on their resumes. Hair color, height, weight, other personal characteristics. Languages spoken. Accents. Special skills. Kind of car you own. You just never know what might peak a casting agent's or producer's interest. Oh, you've got a Boston accent. Perfect, please come for an audition. Oh, you can sing opera or rap or blues or Mongolian rock, come on in. You can blow a shofar? Ride a unicycle? Run a marathon? Play a tuba? Race sled dogs? Come in. You've got bowhunting skills, nun chuck skills, computer hacking skills, we want to see you.

Or in my case, your wife's got a Basset Hound, you're the man—or dog—for us.

"The PBS people must have seen me in *Romeo and Juliet*," I told Anna as I hung up the phone. "It would explain why they want Maggie for the show."

The next day, I called the producer and told her that Maggie would take the role.

Maggie was a rescue dog. She'd rescued Anna.

Two years earlier, Anna was depressed, having just miscarried. Then, our dog, Andy, died. Though we still had Wenny, our big, beautiful

Saint Bernard, it was just too much. One morning, as I helped our daughter, Grace, get ready for school, I made a decision.

After Grace got on the school bus, I called the farm where I'd got Wenny about a year earlier. It was a working farm that also bred Saint Bernards. I'd surprised Anna with Wenny the puppy for Anna's birthday. I'll surprise her again. When I called, I learned they didn't have any Saint litters, but they did have a whole bunch of Basset Hound pups. Why would they breed such ridiculous looking little hound dogs when they bred magnificent, majestic Saint Bernards, I inquired.

"Because," Maura, the woman who ran the farm said on the phone, "they're both wonderful family dogs."

That's all I needed to hear. The next morning, I kept Grace out of school so that she could go with me. On that chilly November day, Maura led us into the heated barn, where there were more than a dozen delightful Basset pups bopping around inside a pen.

"What do you think?" I asked Grace after we watched the pups for ten minutes.

"That one," she said, pointing at a puppy who was standing on two or three others. She was the most energetic, crazy little whirlwind in the lot. Grace carried the pup in her lap as I drove us home.

On the way, Grace started to cry. Andy had died only a few weeks earlier, and perhaps it was too soon to get another dog. Had I made a mistake? Did we all needed to grieve longer?

At home, I tip-toed into the master bedroom. "We have something for you." I opened the bedroom door and motioned for Grace to come in. She slipped the little puppy, warm and soft as velvet, under the covers next to Anna. Anna's recuperation began almost immediately. It was truly love at first snuggle.

Anna later named the pup Maggie because the pup stole anything she could, just like a magpie. Socks, a wallet, a shiny set of keys, anything could end up under her bed. Even better if she could get you to chase her first in a vain effort to retrieve the stolen item. For one so low and so long, she was amazingly fleet on her stubby feet. I'd only catch her if she tripped on her ears, which she did often. They were so long, they trailed along the floor as she ran.

But what a little devil that magpie was. Of the dogs I've had over the years, Maggie was the most willful. The sweetest yet the most defiant. That defiance, somehow, was part of her charm. Maggie did what she wanted to do when she wanted to do it. I loved that about her.

On the day of the Darwin PBS shoot, Anna and I drove Maggie and Wenny to the park where their scene was to be filmed. They seemed excited to be going to their acting debut, I thought, although it may have been excitement at the chance to pee on a freshly mown field, sniff the posteriors of numerous other dogs, and enjoy a little sunshine.

Upon arrival, we were directed to a hilly green field. The director explained that he wanted all thirty or so dogs to run down the hill together in the scene. The shot would show this crazy scramble of dozens of different dog breeds, from little, tiny pocket dogs to a goofy flat-nosed pug, to insanely long dogs, like Maggie, to huge dogs, like Wenny. And every size and shape in between, all in the same shot. Anna took Wenny up the hill on leash for the shot while I took Maggie. Upon command from the director, the owners and their leashed dogs all went barreling down the hill.

Immediately after the scene was shot, the director asked if Maggie and I could come with him for a special scene. We followed him to the top of the hill. There, he pointed down to the cameraman, who was at the bottom of the hill, a chunky heavy camera resting on top of one of his shoulders.

"OK," the director said, "in this scene, we want your Basset to look off into the distance, a little forlornly, and hold the pose, while the cameraman runs up the hill filming her. Can she do that?" the director asked. "Can you have her hold the pose while she looks forlornly off into the distance?"

"Are you insane?" I asked, "you've clearly never had a dog, have you? Or at least certainly not a hound dog. The good news is, she *always* looks forlorn. But the bad news is, she does what she wants, when she wants, if she feels like it."

It was true. Just six months earlier, Maggie had flunked out of school. I'd enrolled her in a training program, dropped her off in the morning, then picked her up after work. She'd be trained how to walk on leash, respond to simple commands, like sit, stay, come here, and stop chewing my expensive Italian leather wallet with the now soggy paper bills inside.

Only, when I went to pick her up one day, the trainer explained he just couldn't do a thing with her.

"I've been training dogs for nigh on thirty years," he said, "but I ain't never seen no dog like this. She just won't do nothing I say, no matter what."

I was disappointed. But somehow, quietly smiling inside. That's our girl, the rebel. Sticking it to the man again. Making her own rules. Wasn't that the story of my own life, too, I'd thought.

"What am I supposed to tell my wife?" I asked the trainer.

He screwed up his beady eyes as he scratched his scraggly brown beard, then, offered, "well, why don't you tell her Maggie's comin' home. And Hell is comin' with her!"

"So, you see," I explained to the director, as Maggie and I stood atop the hill, the gusty wind twirling her foot long ears like a pair of dancing cornstalks, "I've never been able to get her to do anything. I suppose, really, I've never been able to get any girl, canine or human, to do anything."

"Huh?" the director said, clearly puzzled. He only asked for me to make Maggie look forlornly off into the distance and to hold the pose. Not for my life story.

Later that year, Anna and I bristled with excitement the night that the PBS Darwin special was to be aired on TV. As we relaxed on our sofa, with Grace and Maggie and Wenny and popcorn—Maggie's preference was for kettle corn—the show began. About halfway through, the dog scene came on. To our surprise, the scene was in slow motion. As thirty plus dogs ever so slowly descended the grassy hill, there was majestic Wenny, her enormous Saint Bernard jowls slowly flapping up and down. And there, too, was Maggie, her ears taking flight in the artificially slow breeze. She looked a little like *The Flying Nun* would look if Sally Field had been a Basset Hound.

There I was, too, in my first big time, breakthrough acting role!

"Do you see it?" I asked Anna.

"See what?"

"Right there, look, on screen, to the right of Maggie. That's *me*. I mean, that little patch of blue—that's my sneaker. It's my left foot."

"How can you tell?" Anna asked.

"Because," I explained, see that big hole in the toe? That's where Maggie chewed clean through. I'm telling you, no doubt about it, it's Wenny, Maggie, and my left foot. We're famous."

A month later, a letter from PBS arrived in the post. It contained a check for five hundred dollars for Maggie's and Wenny's day on the set. To this day, many years later, that's still four hundred dollars more than I ever made for an acting gig. I thought about framing the check and proudly—or, perhaps, sheepishly—displaying it on our living room wall. But then I thought, no. Maggie had saved Anna's life. How would Maggie want to use the money?

The next day, after work, I hugged Anna and Grace in our kitchen. "I could use a hand with the groceries, Grace," I said.

"Sure, Dad," she replied.

I loved the look on Grace's face as she helped me carry in fifty boxes of Milk Bones dog biscuits. That was the girls' payment, except for a small amount I reserved to buy a new pair of sneakers. I took the sneaker Maggie had chewed a hole in and I hung it on the wall of our den, where it remains to this day.

Maggie passed on a few years ago, just before the start of the pandemic. I'll never take that sneaker down. It's a tribute to the hound who saved Anna's life, and, however fleetingly, made me a star. Or, at least, my left foot.

●

I once was the Chief Operating Officer of the hippiest business in America. One chilly gray November morning, I stood in front of Boston Harbor Periodicals. I'd received a call from an executive recruiter who knew from our business relationship that I was always interested in writing (although I'd gone into business as a career), and that I'd worked in operations at newspapers, marketing agencies, and so on. Now he had a client in magazine publishing for me to meet. I stood on a street in Boston, facing a tall black steel door on the side of a squat brick building. I was there for an interview but thought I must be in the wrong place. No business name on the building. No marquee. Just "777 Morton Avenue" spray-painted in white on the black door. I opened the door and walked inside.

I was now standing in a tiny room with a steel staircase going up, a handrail on the brick wall, and nothing else. No lobby. No neatly attired businesspeople milling about conducting, well, business. As I placed a foot on the first step of the metal tread, it groaned under my weight, even though I only weighed one hundred eighty pounds. I grabbed the handrail with my gloved right hand, and, as I gave it a slight tug to begin ascending the stairs, the retaining bolt that affixed the bottom of the rail to the brick wall popped out and clattered onto the stone floor. I stood for a moment, considering turning around and leaving. Although I was glad to be interviewing with a magazine publisher, I started to wonder just what kind of magazines these folks published. Still, I thought, I'm here, might as well have the interview.

At the top of the stairs, several floors up, was a plain wooden door. It opened onto a capacious but ramshackle place. There were desks and bookcases and magazine racks, throw rugs and lava lamps and hanging beads, plants and bicycles and guitars, strewn about here and there. And there were people. Colorfully, casually dressed people. Bearded people. Beaded people. Reading, writing, playing guitars, smoking things, drinking, and laughing. I walked over to a man sitting in a cross-legged yoga position on a throw rug, apparently smoking a Marijuana cigarette.

"Hey, man," he said, looking up at me through his rose-colored spectacles. From the astonished look on his hairy face, I thought he'd never seen a man in a business suit in person.

"Hey to you," I replied. "I'm looking for the publisher."

"Beats me," he said, shrugging his shoulders. But then, looking up, I saw a man sitting in the only office on the floor. I walked over and knocked on the office door. The publisher, Chris Kraven, waved for me to come in. He was sitting at his desk, which was littered with papers, and eating a bagel. I could see he was tall although he was seated. He was thin, with short hair, round horn-rimmed glasses, a white dress shirt, and a bow tie. He looked like a prissy skinny chicken in a bow tie.

"So, you're the business guy," he said, then pecked at his bagel. "That's great. We need discipline," he added, then *pecked pecked pecked* at the bagel.

"Well, I'm certainly disciplined," I said.

"Good. You're hired," he said. *Peck, peck, peck.*

"Thank you," I said. "Is there a plan?"

"We have two magazines. *Chef's Illustrated* does four million in revenue and makes a gross profit of one million a year. It has no advertising. All the revenue is from subscriptions. I've grown the subscription base as much as I can. The other magazine, *Naturally Healthy*, has advertising revenue, but also costs much more to produce and loses a lot of money. My plan to is replicate *Chef's* with other ad-free highly profitable magazines. Like maybe *Wood Illustrated*. If we have a second mag doing four million in revenue and one million in profit, we'll then have a total of two million in profits. Then if we add a third illustrated mag—"

"Wait, wait, don't tell me," I interrupted, "then you'd have, let me do the math, two, then add the one, yes, yes, that would be three million. And then a fourth mag and that would be, let's see now, take three, add the one—four million?"

Chris finally stopped shuffling papers and looked up at me. His little black beady junglefowl eyes stared at my face intensely, studying. Then he combed his wattle with his right hand, looked up at me, and said, "man, you're *good!*"

The next day was my first as the new Chief Operating Officer. The two important things I did that day were to let half the staff go, then hire a new financial controller. I didn't fire anyone. They let themselves go. Chris called a company staff meeting. A few dozen people gathered in the center of the floor, sitting in chairs, on rugs, one even in a cloth swing suspended from the ceiling. Chris introduced me to everyone. He explained that I was there to help the place "run like a business."

"The first thing we need," I informed the group," is office hours. Right now, no one knows when any other colleague will be in, because people come to work when they feel like it. From now on, we're going to be open from nine to five, Monday to Friday. And everyone needs to be here then."

"I have a question," a woman sitting on a blue and red braided rug said. "Does that have to be 9:00 a.m? Or is 9:00 p.m. good?"

"9:00 a.m.," I said, "that's in the morning."

"No way, man!" she exclaimed. Then she stood up and stormed out the door. I never saw her again. To this day I'm not sure what she did at the company. No one else seemed to know, either.

I asked the group if there were any other questions.

"What if I can't start until later in the morning because of my aura?" a man in blue jeans, and a tie-dye tee shirt with the catchy phrase "Stick it to the Man" on front, and a red and blue bead necklace, asked. "My aura shines brightest around 11:30 a.m.," he said.

I didn't know much about auras. Only that they were believed to be energy fields which emanated from spiritual people, and which glowed in pretty hues of blue or pink or red. Possibly green.

"I'm here to help make our company profitable and to grow the business," I explained, "I'm more concerned about the color of money than the color of your aura."

With that, he immediately stood up and exited the building, neither he nor his aura ever to be seen again. It went on like that for a while that first day, until about half the staff left. It worked out well, though, as the half who remained appeared to be the people who worked. I learned later that Boston Harbor Periodicals was the successor to a religious institute founded decades earlier in the same building. A Hindu religious leader, Swami Someone-or-Other, founded a school there to pass on the true knowledge to disciples. One disciple eventually started a newsletter for his followers. She was one of the reasons I needed a new Controller. The newsletter woman eventually became the Controller of the Swami's school, and later of Boston Harbor Periodicals. But she had no accounting or financial background. She'd originally gone to study with the Swami. But since she could add numbers, the Swami put her in charge of accounting. She only liked to send invoices when "the time was *right*" she told me. She also left after hearing that we were now going to have rules.

Such were the seeds of what was now Boston Harbor Periodicals. Only now the publisher, and an investor in the business, the man who founded White Elephant Farms, were not all that interested in the true knowledge. They were after something a little earthlier.

My next move, in the afternoon of my first day on the new job, was to call Lisa C. I needed financial help. Like yesterday. Lisa and I had worked together at my last company, a newspaper, where I was the Chief Operating Officer, and she was the Controller. Like me, she was a businessperson. She was an accounting wizard, not to mention very calm and sensible, and she was used to commonsense business procedures and rules. She didn't suffer fools. She'd grown up in America's heartland, I think on a farm, I suppose where she learned to count chickens and whatnot. Later, she went to college for accounting. Looking around the magazine office that afternoon, at the braided rugs and chair swings and lava lamps and reefer butts, I smiled as I picked up my desk phone to call Lisa to offer her the job of Controller. This was going to be good!

Lisa's first and nearly last day started the next morning. Sitting at her desk, as she poured through the company's financial records, she looked up at me.

"You know the woman who was the Controller before me, what was her name, Flower, or Possum, or Petunia? Well, I don't think she understood accounting," Lisa said.

"Why, what's wrong?" I said.

"We're broke. We take in less than we spend. We probably have enough funds for another month."

There was a moment of silence. Then something happened. Something unexpected and rare: I had an epiphany.

"What if," I said, "we can get Chris on television? People love quirky chefs. Just think of *The Frugal Gourmet*, *The French Chef*, etc. Maybe we can set up a kitchen here, and feature Chris, in all his peckish ways, testing different products and recipes. A sort of reality TV cooking show?"

"That's brilliant!" Lisa said. "And he can have special guests, like on some of those other cooking shows. You know, Elmo or Itzhak Perlman."

"No, not Perlman—he's already been a guest on *The Frugal Gourmet*" I pointed out.

"OK, no problem," Lisa said, "then maybe Yo-Yo-Ma. There's just one problem," she noted. "We don't have a kitchen. Or the budget for one."

"No worries," I said, "I've got some contacts in the theater district in town. I'll get a few set designers and we'll have a kitchen set made, like on Broadway. Then I'll talk to Howie, next door, at the deli. He can do the cooking part off camera when we need a real oven, then just bring the cooked food here between takes. He makes a killer black whole pastrami sandwich."

Lisa looked a little troubled.

"You know," I assured her, "*The French Chef* isn't French. And *The Frugal Gourmet* drives a Mercedes."

And thus, the plan for what was ultimately to become one of the hottest cooking shows on cable TV—*America's Test Chicken*—was hatched. Advertisers flocked to buy in (no pun intended). And the money was rolling in, too. Turns out that the test we had for *Wood Illustrated* was a dud. So, we dropped Chris's idea of more magazines and instead launched the new TV show. Boston Harbor Periodicals was saved.

That *America's Test Chicken* launch was almost thirty years ago. Today, my good friend Lisa is retired. She lives on a farm in western, MA, with her husband, her dog, and fifty chickens. I live in the suburbs of Boston, with my dog, my son, and his five Rhode Island Red hens. My son loves country music. One of his favorite songs is Johnny Cash's *A Boy Named Sue*. And one of his favorite chickens is a girl named Chris.

●

The Seventh Sense

Did you ever wake up at the crack of dawn to find Bruce Willis, naked from head to toe, bald as a newborn baby, as mad as a bull, standing by the foot of your bed? I have. He looked as if he'd walked straight off the set of *Die Hard* into my bedroom.

"Feingold," he said, "wake up! Why do you keep putting me in your stories? What's up with that? Some sick, twisted man-crush?"

I was disoriented. I sat up in bed, thought for a moment, then asked, "which stories? Do you mean *Nowhere Man*? That's about The Frugal Gourmet and Itzhak Perlman. You're not in it. The one after that was *America's Test Chicken*, but that was about Chris Kraven, the guy from the TV show *America's Test Chicken*."

Bruce rolled his eyes and leaned menacingly towards me. "The stories about Russia, bro, when your driver says 'you luke like Bruce Villis.' You don't look anything like me!"

It was true. I'm tall, thin, of slight frame, blond, and with the finely structured nose, chin, and cheekbones of a European. This can't be right, I thought. Just then, I decided to pinch my forearm hard to see if this was a dream. I pinched, and then I looked over again at the foot of my bed. No Bruce Willis. The blood I'd seen on my hand, and the searing pain I'd felt in the roof of my mouth, were also gone. I'd just awoken from a nightmare about surgery I'd had thirty years earlier. The day before this nightmare, I'd met with the same surgeon who, so long ago, excised a large piece of flesh from the roof of my mouth and sewed it in strips over the receding gums of my upper front teeth.

"If it won't stop bleeding," the doctor had said as I sat bleeding in the operating chair in his periodontal office, "suck on a tea bag." For weeks, I tasted the murky mixture of blood, saliva and Darjeeling, as the gaping wound on my palette healed as quickly as an amoeba swimming from one side of the Atlantic Ocean to the other.

Now, the day before the nightmare, I was back in Dr. Pane's office, as he inspected my gums. One week earlier, my dentist informed me that it was time again to consider gum grafts. "Wouldn't it be easier," I'd asked my dentist, "if I just slit my wrists and bled out?"

"There are some new procedures since you last had surgery," he replied. "Dr. Pane (spelled like 'pane' but pronounced like 'pain,' a terrifically horrible yet true name for my periodontist), will explain it all to you."

"That sounds like the title for my first graphic horror novel," I noted. "*Dr. Pane Will Explain It All to You*, a graphic horror novel by Jeffrey M. Feingold. Published posthumously after his death—from gum surgery."

"Oh, nothing to worry about," my dentist assured me.

"What, me worry?" I asked.

The next week, as I sat in Dr. Pane's Chair of Pain, my mouth as wide open as an angry hippopotamus, as he poked with cold pointy instruments of torture the places at the bottom of my teeth where there should be gum but was now only nerves and pain, he offered this astounding periodontal news:

"We can still do the same procedure we did for you last time, but because of the pain and bleeding, most patients opt for the latest procedure."

"Mum mum grrr grrr ra ra," I said.

"What did you say?" he asked, removing his ice pick from my mouth.

"I said, that's great! I can't do the same thing again; it took a month to heal, and I can't be off the grid that long now. So, what's the new option?"

"We use tissue harvested from the departed," he said.

"Wait," I said, "you're going to put parts from the deceased in me?"

He looked at me, deadpan, and clarified: "yup."

"From people who bought the farm?" I asked with disbelief. "People who are pushing up daisies? Who have gone to meet their maker? Who have been laid to rest? Who are out of commission? Who are six feet under? Who are ... *dead*?"

"I know," he said, "it can seem a little strange. But it's all from donors. And the tissue is dead and fully sterilized."

"Well, I'm glad it's from donors," I noted. "I'm glad it's not extracted from people forcibly, against their will while still alive. Still, it just seems, well—*creepy*."

"Up to you," he said. "But there's close to no pain this way, since we don't have to remove a large piece of tissue from your palette."

I felt between a rock and very hard place. I'd either submit to a month of excruciating pain, or have dead people inserted into me. But I knew the former was out of the question. Not because I'm chicken, though who loves intense pain? But because I couldn't be out of commission for the extended recovery required with the palette process. So, I agreed to join the dead-beat club.

I signed some forms for the doctor before leaving his office. One was an agreement to pay for the procedure. The other was some release of liability. I guess if it all went wrong and I kicked the bucket, my surviving family wouldn't be able to sue him. But he would be able to donate my gums.

The next morning, I woke up to Bruce Willis, as previously described. But the real problem was that evening. That's when the trouble began. Flipping through the channels of the large screen TV in my living room, I came across the movie *The Sixth Sense*, part way through. Watching the scene in which Cole, played by Haley Joel Osment, says "I see dead people" to the psychologist played by Bruce Willis, something in my brain got re-wired. My gum surgery was scheduled for a few days later. But I just knew I couldn't go through with it.

That night, I went to sleep after turning off the movie. It was August, very hot, bedroom windows open, air heavy and thick. I awoke in a sweat in the night to find Bruce Willis at the foot of my bed yet again. Only this time he had hair, and a tie, and clothes. Thank God for that, I thought. He was dressed as the doctor from *The Sixth Sense*.

"I'm here to help you." He spoke slowly, in a soft, gentle, un-Willis like voice, just as he did in *The Sixth Sense*.

"You *can't* help me," I said. "No one can."

"Why not," he gently inquired.

"Because—I taste dead people. Only they don't know they're dead. And they don't know what they taste like."

"What is that" he asked quietly.

"Chicken," I said. "They taste like chicken."

"Is that so bad?" he asked.

"Yes," I explained. "I'm a vegetarian. If they tasted like peppers, or maybe apples, that might be OK."

I started to pinch my forearm hard again. Then I looked up. He had vanished. Before I could even tell him that he, too, tasted like chicken and that, therefore, just as in the movie, he must already be dead. I rose, went to my kitchen, where I had enough sense to drink six glasses of Cabernet Franc. Then went back to sleep.

The next morning, I called Dr. Pane's office to cancel the surgery.

"Why are you canceling?" the doctor's assistant asked.

"Because I'm a vegetarian," I said.

I've never had gum surgery since. And I've never eaten a chicken. And I've never watched another re-rerun of *The Sixth Sense*.

●

The Water Witch

My father didn't believe in witches or magic wands. He was a man of science. But other than watching *Star Trek* every Friday night, or gazing at the stars though his chunky telescope, my Dad most loved gardening. He was born and raised in downtown Boston, a city kid through and through. Then, when I was eight years old, he and my mother bought their first house, in the suburbs, where my Dad discovered his love of all things green. Dad often talked about his dream of moving to Israel to help turn sand into farmland. For now, though, his Negev Desert was our big backyard where, just as in the desert, water was scarce. Every summer our town had a watering ban. Watering his plump red tomatoes, shiny purple-black eggplants, and emerald green peppers was limited to certain days and hours of the week, and then only by handheld hose. How was he to turn dust into arable land without water? Some men may simply have given up. But Dad, being a man of science, made the logical decision: dig a well.

I stood in our yard one sunny summer Sunday, bristling with anticipation as I awaited all manner of scientists and heavy equipment to come turn our dry backyard into a fertile field of green. I imagined men and women in white lab coats, with glass beakers for testing soil, thick lab goggles, and lots of fun equipment, including giant earth-moving drills to bore down deep into the earth's core—all the way to China if necessary. I was always dragging around a pillowcase full of firecrackers and cherry bombs and such, and I pictured myself working together with the well crew for some of the trickier demolition work. I was practically jumping out of my skin with anticipation.

Just then, a diminutive red pickup truck puttered into our driveway. The engine spluttered and coughed and finally gave its last mournful gasp. I read the words painted in white on the driver's door:

Wally's Wells
And just below that, the memorable tagline:
Where Wally goes …
water flows

A tall, portly man stepped out onto the driveway and slammed the truck door closed. He squinted down at me with little black-eyed pea pupils peering out from a pudgy, pasty potato face. He wore a red plaid shirt, and overalls smudged with dirt. In his right hand he gripped a long stick shaped like the letter Y. I kept peering my head around past the back of the truck to see if the heavy equipment and scientists were arriving. But alas, there was only Wally.

"Mister, how are you gonna dig a well with that pointy stick?" I inquired.

"This stick is special," he said. "It's called a divining rod or watch witch. It'll tell me where the water is. Once I find the water, then we'll come in with heavy equipment to drill."

"That's where I can help," I offered, handing him a round red cherry bomb I'd just pulled out of my pillowcase demolition bag. I guess he hadn't seen one before because he held it up to his broad nose, sniffed a few times, then began shaking it violently.

"Be careful, Mister," I hollered, "you can blow your hand clean off with one of those!"

Just then, my father walked out our front door and over to the truck. As he and Mister Wally shook hands—luckily Wally still had both of his—my Dad kept peering around toward the back of the pickup truck. I guess he, too, was wondering when the scientists would be arriving.

"It's just—you?" Dad asked haltingly.

"Yessiree," Wally said with a broad, yellow-toothed smile, "but don't worry none. Where Wally goes—water flows!"

My Dad looked worried. We all walked into the backyard. Wally explained that, since it's so expensive to dig, he came first to find the right spot. My Dad must have been getting bothered by mosquitos, because he kept gently slapping his forehead with the palm of his hand as Wally ambled about the yard with the bottom of the divining rod pointed straight ahead as he held the two shorter sections in his meaty paws.

"You sure have a lot of holes in your yard," he noted to my Dad.

"Rabbits," Dad said, "we've got them everywhere."

"Bingo!" Wally exclaimed, as he stopped slowly ambulating and spread his tree-trunk legs directly over a rabbit hole. As he hummed quietly to himself, the divining rod began to slowly rise, moving in an arc from its position pointing straight ahead until it pointed directly at the sky as Wally held it over his curly cabbage red hair.

"It's here," he said. "I can feel it."

"Rabbits?" my father asked, hitting his forehead with the palm of his right hand.

"Nope," said Wally. "It's H2O. That's water to you gents, but to me it's an inorganic, transparent, tasteless, odorless and colorless chemical compound which is the main constituent of the Earth's hydrosphere and the fluids of all known living organisms."

If my father's jaw fell any further to the ground, I feared it would have slipped right into the rabbit hole. He put his left hand on Wally's shoulder while he shook hands with him with his right, and asked, "so, when do we drill?"

"Sunup tomorrow," Wally said. He took a little orange flag on a metal wire out of his overall pocket and stuck it into the ground right next to the rabbit hole.

As Dad and Wally headed over to Wally's truck, I peered down the bone-dry rabbit hole. I could see a fair way down into the dusty sandy hole. I had a funny feeling in my stomach.

That night, a bearded man came to me in my dreams. He floated above me. He wore a flowing white robe, brown leather open toe sandals, and he carried a wooden staff. I thought he must be Moses. But he was surrounded by animals, each in pairs, all floating around him. Pairs of goats, sheep, rabbits, and many more animals, circling around and around and around.

"Son of David," his voice boomed, "a great flood shall come forth, into these your father's fields. But lo, for this to happen, you must mark my words and heed my instructions. Only then shall this barren land become fertile."

I had never met Moses. Still, he looked a lot like Charlton Heston in *The Ten Commandments*. But I wondered, what's up with all the animals?

"Are you sure this will work?" I inquired.

He cocked his head quizzically to the side and glowered down at me. Then he raised his staff to the heavens and said, *behold*! Looking up, I saw clouds part and a vast expanse of verdant farmland appear. Then he told me what I must do.

"Heed my words, child, and the waters shall flow. Now go forth as I command you. No more questions! Oh, just one more thing—don't call me Moses."

I tried to go back to sleep. After tossing and turning a few hours, I arose in my pajamas. I took the flashlight from my nightstand drawer, then opened my bedroom window. I climbed down the oak tree into the backyard. With the flashlight, I found the orange flag in the blackness. I then dragged the garden hose from the spigot on the back of the house and stuck the end of the hose as far down the rabbit hole as I could. Then I walked back to the house again and turned the spigot handle on as far as it would go. I could hear the water flowing, even though Wally wasn't there. I left the spigot on and climbed back up the tree and into my bedroom. I set my Timex watch alarm for five in the morning, a half an hour before sunrise, and just five hours from the moment I crawled back under my sheets and closed my eyes.

When the *bleep-bleep-bleep* of my Timex woke me, I again took the flashlight, opened my bedroom window, and descended the oak tree. I turned off the spigot, dragged the hose back to the house, and then climbed back up the oak.

That morning, after breakfast, I heard Wally's pickup truck as it spluttered and coughed and gasped its way into our driveway. This time he wasn't alone. A man driving a sort of pile driving truck pulled into the driveway, drove around Wally's pickup and my Dad's Ford LTD sedan, and over to the hole marked with the orange flag. Wally, Dad and I walked over to watch as the pile driving man began pulverizing the ground with a percussion cable. Within seconds of pulverizing, water began seeping up and pooling. The ground was saturated from my nighttime shenanigans. Standing on the sopping earth, Wally looked at his divining rod, clutched in his right hand, then over to my Dad.

"By God, man, I've done it!" Wally shouted to my Dad over the roar of the percussion driver. He kept looking at his divining rod, holding it at a distance and turning it slowly over and over, perhaps trying to ascertain how it had miraculously transformed from a dead branch of a hazel tree into a living, mystical instrument of the gods.

Just then I had a terrible thought. Had I drowned the rabbits? But then Wally tapped my Dad's arm and said, "look there," as he pointed at a whole bunch of rabbits lined up at the far end of the yard. They appeared to be watching us intently, and—I thought—chuckling.

●

I Walk The Line

Part 1: To Infinity and Beyond

Mrs. Snapples drew a white chalk line from one end of the green chalkboard to the other. God, how I adored her. I was sure we would get married, have ten, maybe twenty babies, just as soon as I finished third grade, got a job, and could afford to get babies delivered from wherever one orders them.

The rectangular chalkboard ran the length of the wall behind her desk at the front of her third-grade classroom at the Emily A. Fifield Elementary School in Boston.

"Where does the line end?" Mrs. Snapples asked, turning her comely face to the class, clapping chalk dust from delicate Snow-White hands.

One of my two hands, disproportionality large for my age, with beanstalk-long fingers, shot up straighter and faster than an arrow. I was ready to explode out of my wooden desk chair.

"Yes, Jeffrey," she said, "what do *you* think?"

"It ends right *there!*" I exclaimed, pointing to the end of the chalk line. "Can't *you* see? It ends at the—*end.*"

"No," she gently suggested, "it does not."

"What do you mean? I can see the end as plain as the nose on your face."

"There is no end," she declared, rather smugly, but no matter: the line may have ended at the end of the chalkboard, but my love for Mrs. Snapples was unending.

"No end!" I cried, *"no end?"*

"Yes, it goes on forever," she added.

I looked again at the entire length of the chalk line. On the right side, there was a beginning, then there was a long middle, then far away on the left there was an abrupt end. Just like life. You're born, you live nearly forever, or until you're old—maybe forty years if you're lucky—then you die. The end.

"Yes, there's no end," she said. "That's called *infinity*," she said, "because the line is *infinite*."

My eager beanstalks shot up again.

"Yes, Jeffrey?"

"May I approach the bench, your Honor?" I asked. My grandfather and I watched *Court TV* every day after school.

"Yes, Jeffrey," Mrs. Snapples said with a smile, "you may."

I arose from my chair at the front of the class—I liked being teacher's pet—and walked over to Mrs. Snapples. Her perfume was to die for. It might have been dandelions or earthworms or some such scent intoxicating to robins and third grade boys. The scent went so well with her sunflower yellow dress and her long hair as black as sunflower eyes.

"Here," I said, holding up my black plastic frame glasses with Coke-bottle-thick lenses to her. I was blind without them. "You need this way more than me," I explained.

"That's thoughtful of you, Jeffrey," she said, "but just because you can't *see* something doesn't mean it's not real. That's called *Science*."

I pondered. Things were getting deep.

"Mrs. Snapples," I finally said, "my Ukrainian grandfather says just because you *want* to see something doesn't make it real. He says that's called *Life*."

"He sounds like he's a very nice man. Is he a teacher?"

"No, he's a butcher."

"That's OK," Mrs. Snapples noted. "Mahatma Gandhi said that all work is noble."

"I don't know him," I said, "is he a butcher, too?"

"No, he was a vegetarian, a great thinker, and a lover of peace."

"Well, I'm not a lover of peas," I noted, "so I'd rather be a butcher."

Her black sunflower seed eyes narrowed, and her face contracted. "Why is that?" she said.

"Because I don't like peas. But a black pastrami and mustard on a bulkie roll will last you all day, although I don't like the dill pickles. My grandfather says lunch is the most important meal of the day. My grandfather is wise. He's old, I think over forty!"

"I see, well, Jeffrey, why don't you take your seat? One more thing—do you think you understand now where the line ends?"

"For sure!" I cried. "It ends right *there*," I added, pointing, "at the end of the chalkboard. You really should try my glasses, Mrs. Snapples." I took my seat.

That day, I decided it was the end of the line for me, as far as math was concerned. I mean, who needs it? It just didn't make any sense. I decided I would grow up to be a famous writer. I'd live and write nearly forever, maybe until I was forty, in a nursing home, so old I'd be unable to remember how much I loved black pastrami and mustard sandwiches on bulkie rolls.

"There's a line directly from God," Rabbi Hoffman said, facing the class of third graders in the after-school Hebrew class at the synagogue my family belonged to. "It's not a line you can see. And it's a line that ends here, in my heart." He pointed to his chest.

Oh no, here we go *again*. I rolled my eyes and moaned loudly while holding my stomach. *What is it* with you adult people and lines?

"Is there something wrong, Jeffrey?" the Rabbi asked, thoughtfully stroking his long gray beard, "are you ill?"

He cocked his head quizzically to one side. He looked concerned, and like an owl, a concerned wise old owl.

"No," I explained, "it's just that Mrs. Snapples said the line goes on forever."

"Which line? The line from God?" the Rabbi asked.

"I don't know," I said, "I'm so confused. See, there's this line at the end of her chalk—."

"I see," the Rabbi interrupted, "well, I don't think I know Mrs. Snapples. The line of which I speak is the line that starts from *God*." He looked up at the ceiling.

I looked up, too, but couldn't see God or even a line. Only a white popcorn-plaster ceiling with little cracks here and there between the recessed fluorescent lights. Perhaps the line came from God through one of the little cracks? But I thought the line ended at the end of the chalkboard in Mrs. Snapples' class? How did it get from her classroom up to God, then from God down to the Rabbi's heart? Or did it travel in the other direction? Maybe the Rabbi needed to borrow my glasses, too?

"And that line," the Rabbi repeated, "goes all the way from God right into my heart." He pointed his stubby right index finger at the left side of his chest.

Rabbi Hoffman went on to explain that the line of which he spoke went straight from God into his heart as it does for all our people, the Jewish people, "because we're God's Chosen People." I was just starting Hebrew School, so I didn't know all the facts. But I did know that some people believed there was a guy named Jesus who chose *them*, and other people believed in a guy named Muhammed who chose *them*, and still other people who believed other things. Once, after school, Grandfather and I watched a movie about people who wore cool shiny clothes and jewelry and believed there was a great cat god in the sky who chose them.

The Rabbi said that long ago God decided to choose our people to be his favorite people. My troublesome hand shot up in the air yet again.

"Yes," Rabbi Hoffman asked, "you have a question?"

"How do we know that we're the Chosen People, if everyone who isn't Jewish thinks, they're the Chosen People? And if the line ends in Mrs. Snapples' classroom, how does it get up to God and then down to you?"

There was a pause. Then the Rabbi slowly raised his right index finger, opened his mouth, then closed it again as he slowly lowered his right hand. There was another, even longer pause.

"Wait here, children," he finally said. "I'm going to go to my office to make a call."

Driving home from Hebrew School with my Dad, in his snazzy black Ford LTD with slippery red vinyl seats, there were a few moments of silence. I inhaled deeply, delighting in that new vinyl smell. Then my Dad said, "Son, I'm going to take you out of Hebrew school for now. I don't think they're ready."

And just like that, it was the end of the line. The line which, I guess, went from Mrs. Snapples' chalkboard, up to God, down to Rabbi Hoffman's heart, then over to my Dad, courtesy of AT&T.

●

The Wrong Napkin

My maternal grandfather was a Jewish mobster at the turn of the 20th century. My sisters and I never knew him. He was murdered before we were born. Rubbed out in his prime. At least, that's what we'd heard. He was killed by the Jewish mob. 'Rubbed out' because our people didn't run around "whacking" their adversaries (we were a civil people, after all. We simply rubbed them out. You know, like the way mom rubbed out stains on my old blue jeans).

Many years later, when my beloved sister Marion and I yet again grew curious about the dark side of our family history, we did some research. I obtained a copy of our grandfather's death certificate. I'd made arrangements for the certificate to be mailed directly from the U.S. government to my sister's house. A few weeks later, my phone rang.

"Are you sitting down," my sister asked? I sat. "According to his death certificate, Nana's husband was killed by a fruit cart. A runaway fruit cart." But how can that be, we asked each other? We always heard he was a mobster.

"No, it's simple," I reasoned with my sister, "that just must have been how the Jews did it back then." Subtle. No vulgar gunshots or stabbings. Instead, it would be handled delicately. Perhaps some undetectable poison in one's chicken soup. Or a piano cleverly dropped from the fifth floor at the precise moment one's adversary is passing on the sidewalk. Or—or—a runaway cart laden with heavy, deadly, precisely aimed fruit. Passion fruit, no doubt.

Still, it made no sense to us. The quiet secret family story, told in hushed tones so that children wouldn't hear—though of course we always did—was that grandfather was a member of the underworld (I wasn't sure exactly where the underworld was located on a map, but I imagined a vast underground network of tunnels somewhere under the earth's crust).

Jeffrey M. Feingold

And then there was grandfather's wife, our beloved Nana, Frances. Oh, how I adored her! She was a loving grandmother but every bit the mobster's glamorous moll. Tall, pretty, a ballroom dancer with a shock of jet-black hair and an elegant bearing. She was poised, graceful, and stylish. She drove a flashy silver Camaro. And she thought I was the bee's knees. That drove my mother crazy, just as it made me adore Nana even more.

Nana took me everywhere with her. I loved staying over at her place and loved going places with her in her zippy Camaro. I was sure it had been a gift from someone named Bugsy or Fingers.

One summer morning, she took me to her doctor's office, stopping on the way to get ice cream sugar cones. It was August, quite hot, and as we sat in her doctor's waiting room our chocolate ice cream cones started to drip. The waiting room was chockablock full, mostly of older women, with their fancy broaches and colorful dresses, and even older men in natty hound's-tooth sport coats with shiny black dress shoes.

Back then, one dressed up to see the doctor. I certainly didn't want Nana's ice cream to drip on her pretty dress. "I'll get some napkins," I told her, as I jumped up and bounded across the large waiting room to the bathroom on the other side.

In the bathroom there was a large rectangular metal box affixed to the wall. It had a brushed silver metal crank handle, a large open area in bottom front, and a little sign on it, which read, *Feminine Napkins*. As I turned the handle, my heart soared as if I were Arthur having just pulled the sword from its stone. Soon I would be my Nana's savior! I would hurriedly bring her a napkin in the nick of time, sparing her from the terrible embarrassment of dripping chocolate ice cream on her white cotton pencil dress with blue polka dots.

I literally burst forth from the bathroom door, my heart leaping from my chest, as I heroically waved the napkin with my outstretched arm as high as I could reach, while hollering triumphantly to Nana across the waiting room, "Nana, Nana, I've got you a napkin!"

After her examination, we drove to my parent's house in her mobster coupe in stone cold silence.

Later that afternoon, I helped my father tend to his backyard garden. As he watered the plump red tomato plants, he said, "son, we have to talk. A man and a woman are like, well, tomato plants."

I looked at the wet tomatoes, glistening in the summer sun, and I knew instantly that my father must have completely gone off his rocker.

"You see, son, a woman can't make a tomato without some parts from a man. The parts combine and then a new tomato is born. Do you think you understand? I know you wanted to bring your Nana a napkin to be helpful. But son, it was the wrong napkin. You're a good boy. I'm glad we had the talk. Now everything should be clear. Run along now and play."

The world of mobsters and their molls and tomatoes seemed so strange to me, then, as it does now. I was confused. What did tomatoes have to do with napkins, anyway? Oh well, I said, and ran off to play with my friend, Wolfgang. The only thing I knew with clarity and certainty is that someday I would grow up to be Batman. And then no one would dare to mess with my Nana's tomatoes.

●

The World Of Tomorrow

The airplane was hurtling right at me. I thought I was a goner. My life began flashing before my eyes. The many things I would miss. I'd never ask Molly Finkleblatt to the prom. I'd never grow up to be Batman and save my nana from Jewish mobsters. I'd never live to fulfill my destiny. (I had only the vaguest possible sense of my destiny, but I knew it was supposed to have something to do with greatness).

I was six or seven years old that day so very long ago, standing with friends on the sidewalk in Boston just outside my family home. We were all looking up at the sky. There, on the porch of the top floor of the three-floor apartment where my family lived, stood a colossus: my father, the inventor, casting his homemade airplanes down at us like so many thunderbolts cast to earth by Zeus. I felt a *woosh* of hot summer air as the plane grazed my right ear before crashing to the ground next to my new suede Hush Puppy shoes. Yes, a fiery death missed me by only inches!

"Launch another one, Dad," I hollered up at the man in the sky.

A few moments later, a huge paper B-52 came barreling right for the tip of my friend Wolfgang's nose. There's no way he was going to survive this one!

That was my Dad. He was born to invent. Born for greatness. He was first generation American, his father having come to Boston from Ukraine. My grandfather had a little five-and-dime store in Boston. That was his life here. But not to be the life for his son. No, my father's head was in the stars. He knew every star in every constellation. While other kids had ten speed bikes, Dad had ten telescopes.

He was born for space. But when he was still young and full of starry night dreams, before I was born, tragedy would tether his feet to the ground. His mother had terminal cancer and was sent from hospital to die at home. Back then, there was no hospice, and relatively little thought of palliative care. What did they have back then, after all?

Some morphine. Still, she would often wail in pain throughout the night. This caused anguish my father grappled with for the rest of his life. This was all before I arrived on this lonely planet, and to this day I don't know the full story. But what I do know is that after her death, my father put aside his heavenly dreams and instead worked in my grandfather's store. Family was everything. So, his hopes for college were set aside.

But still, he managed to become an inventor. Not just paper airplanes. He learned electrical design. For many years he worked for a firm that did only one thing, one incredibly specialized thing. Designing prototypes for display at world trade shows, such as the *World of Tomorrow* display at the 1967 World's Fair in Montreal.

The World of Tomorrow! What was it like, I often wondered as a kid. And for my whole life. I could only imagine. Later, when I was ten, my parents bought their one and only house, and growing up, my Dad's basement was full of these World's Fair inventions. Cutting-edge, futuristic things of which most people would hardly dare to dream. Things only read about in science fiction novels. Or seen on science fiction TV shows back in the days when programs were all in black and white. Extraordinary, mind-blowing inventions most Americans could hardly imagine. Inventions such as the "Auto-Dialing Telephone." Yup, that's right, my Dad invented it. And as a little kid, I played with it in the basement. It was one of those heavy black desk set phones, like the kind Spencer Tracey used to call Katherine Hepburn in the old black and white movie, "Desk Set." Or maybe she used it to call him.

Either way, there was a slot at the top of my father's invention. Into this slot one would push a credit card size piece of plastic. This card had vertical columns, each with ten little round tabs. In each column, one of the tabs would be removed, leaving a hole, representing one of the digits in a phone number. When the card was inserted into the phone slot, the phone would then dial the pre-programmed number, slowly pushing the punch card back up through the slot into which it had been inserted. All of this took about five painfully long minutes— longer than it would take to just dial the number with your finger using the rotary dial on the phone. And yet, I always imagined the gasps of awe as folks from across the world stood staring at the space age auto-dialing "World of Tomorrow" telephone.

"How could it be? How does it work? It's from the future! What genius has invented this miracle?"

Duh, folks, it was my Dad! *That* genius. The same one who later invented the first music box controller, which synced lights to music. It had a little fancy knob controller on top with a thin circle of gold leafing around it. Loved to play with that one. And a hundred other brilliant things I grew up with playing in the basement.

My mother and father didn't hold on to things forever. The basement full of inventions somehow eventually disappeared. Oh, how I wish I had that phone today! How I wish I could pass it on to his granddaughter, my only daughter. But my parents just didn't understand the value of keeping things. Just once, they planned to have a yard sale. Looking though the things they were planning to sell, I came across the Seder plate we used for family Passovers while I was growing up.

"You can't give this away," I said to my Dad as I held the silver plate, remembering so many now dead relatives who had gathered with us for Passover's past.

"Why, it's not worth anything," he said, "it not real silver, it's just silver plate."

"I'm not talking about monetary value," I said, "but this is the Seder plate I grew up with. Someday I'll have my own children, and this would be something I can give to them from their grandparents."

A pause, then, "well, you can have it if you want it, but it's not worth anything."

He just didn't understand the concept. But I went off to the Navy, and then to college, and somehow the Seder plate disappeared. If only in my youthful foolishness I'd comprehended the importance of securing it.

And today, I do have a child. My father died a year before my daughter was born. How sad I am not to have some of his inventions to pass on to her. She never met her grandfather. He was gone before the miracle of her birth. He has vanished, as have his creations. The things he invented or owned could not replace the man. Not the silver of his Seder plate, nor the gold leaf on the top of his music controller. Silver and gold cannot replace the absence of a doting grandfather. But perhaps they could have been touchstones, somehow connecting his granddaughter to the purity of his light and love. I don't know. I just know all is lost.

Unlike my parents, I have saved boxes full of memories for my child. Shoeboxes full. The stories written by her in second and third grade. The pictures of dance recitals. The wonderful essays she wrote across her early years. But as I whirl threw the September of my years, I've wondered, what else can I leave for her? And so, I've been writing stories. Stories about leaves from my family tree—from her tree. So that she may, however indirectly, get to know those who came before her. It is my hope that she feels that some part of the past—of her past—has been reclaimed.

Life takes the things one loves away, bit by bit. Like my father before me, I may not be here in her world of tomorrow. But someone will remain. And now she will know his story.

●

Jeffrey M. Feingold

The Sugar Thief

My Aunt Millie was a thief. She was large and loving, warm and wonderful. She was a little short, with a build like a potato. A potato with a large crop of curly orange hair on top. She loved conversations, hugs, and children. As a young boy, I loved when she wrapped me in her arms and gave me a big wet smooch on my cheek, leaving on my white-as-snow Eastern European face two perfect red lipstick imprints that Andy Warhol would have envied. Then she'd whisk me into her kitchen and insist on fattening up her skinny nephew with a homemade chopped liver and onion sandwich, glass of whole milk, and homemade macaroons to die for.

Aunt Millie and Uncle Joe lived in a beautiful white three-story house in an upscale Boston neighborhood. They drove an enormous white Cadillac with red leather seats, at a time when Americans drove either a Ford or a Chevy (my father was a confirmed Ford man), unless they were well off, in which case they drove a Cadillac. They summered in Boston and wintered at their home in Florida. Their origins were humble, but Uncle Joe had found success with his television shop. He sold TVs, at a time when one went to a TV shop in order to purchase a TV. There were no big box stores of any kind. If you wanted meat, you went to see the local butcher. If you wanted fruit and vegetables, you went to the local shop for those. And if you wanted one of those new-fangled boxes for family entertainment, you went to see Uncle Joe. The TVs back then had heavy lead glass in front of the tubes inside— the better to separate you from the radioactivity buzzing around the mysterious array of circuits and tubes and whatnot. My, how things have changed!

I admired Uncle Joe and adored Aunt Millie. But the darker truth is that she was often an embarrassment during my teenage years. She had lived through the Great Depression, and later, World War II, and the memory of those dark days was always with her. When we went out for lunch at the local diner, there were always sugar packets in a little ceramic holder on the table when we arrived. But they weren't there by the time we left. Sometimes I would return to our table after a bathroom visit, only to find the sugar had mysteriously disappeared from the table during my brief absence. Worse was when Aunt Millie would open her white leather pocketbook and start putting in the sugar packets, while I was still at the table eating. I would roll my eyes. What an embarrassment—my aunt stealing sugar from the diner! I could have died. In my youthful foolishness I imagined I was always being looked at—and judged—and that the world always cared about me and what I and my foolish old relative was doing. Had Aunt Millie also surreptitiously slipped some of the flatware into her cavernous pocketbook while I wasn't looking, I wondered? Wasn't there another teacup on the table when we'd arrived?

After years of her culinary crimes, I finally asked her why she took sugar packets with her. She explained how rationing had worked during the Depression and later during WWII. No one could buy sugar in unlimited quantities at the market. She would instead take her ration book to the market and exchange one of the stamps in the book for her half pound of sugar. Sugar was the start, but the rationing extended later to coffee, gasoline, butter, canned milk. Even jams, jellies and cooking oil became subject to rationing. Of course, a black market developed, and criminals got involved. I'd always known her sister's husband was a member of the Jewish mob, and as Aunt Millie explained about rationing, I imagined my maternal grandfather bartering in bootlegged butter before he was, later, rubbed out. But that's a subject for a previous story.

Now that I am in the September of my years, how I regret my youthful intolerance. How I wished I hadn't judged my beloved Aunt so harshly for her sweet thievery. But back then, I found all my familial elders embarrassing. They are mostly gone now, dead these many years. If only I could revive them. I pine for missed conversations. I want to greet all my many dead relatives, to welcome them into my house, to sit together with them at my kitchen table, have a cup of coffee, and listen to their stories. To see their eyes and smiles and to hear their sighs and laughter once more. I know they would then have to return to being shades, for life is not for the dead. Still, I want to sit at the kitchen table and listen to my Uncle Joe talk about the latest in black and white televisions, to hear my grandmother Frances' lilting laugh, to listen to my dad explain about how stars are born and how they eventually die and collapse in on themselves into black holes, and to see my Aunt Millie's broad smile and crop of curly orange hair, and to feel only love and admiration when I return to my kitchen table to find all the sugar packets have mysteriously vanished into thin air. And she would be right to take them, for no matter what your success in life, the darkness is still there. I failed to grasp that as a youth. I wish I hadn't been embarrassed by her humanness. I wish I could shake that stupid young man I was by the shoulders and tell him so many things.

●

Acknowledgements

The Black Hole Pastrami originally published by The Pinch Literary Journal

The Buzz Bomb originally appeared in The Ravens Perch Literary Journal

The LTD originally appeared in The Book of Matches Literary Journal

Here's Looking at You Syd first published by Choeofpleirn Press in Glacial Hills Review

My Left Foot originally published by American Writers Review

America's Test Chicken, The Seventh Sense, The Water Witch, and *I Walk the Line* originally appeared in The Wise Owl Literary Magazine

Nowhere Man originally appeared in Past Ten

Avalanche originally published by Impspired Magazine. Also appeared in The Bark.

Grace originally appeared in Hare's Paw Literary Journal

The Wrong Napkin and *The World of Tomorrow* originally appeared in Wilderness House Literary Review

The Sugar Thief and *Goth Girl* originally published in print in Schuylkill Valley Journal

Jeffrey M. Feingold is a writer of fiction in Boston. His stories have been nominated for the Pen America Short Story Prize for Emerging Writers, the Pushcart Prize, and The Best American Short Stories; finalist for the 2022 Eyelands Book Awards; shortlisted for the 2022 Exeter Story Prize in England; and winner of London's Superlative literary journal annual short story prize.

Jeffrey's work appears in magazines, such as the international *Intrepid Times*, and in *The Bark* (a national magazine with readership over 250,000). Jeffrey's work has also been published in anthologies, and by numerous literary reviews and journals, including *The Pinch, Maudlin House, Wilderness House Literary Review, Meat for Tea, Schuylkill Valley Journal*, and elsewhere. Jeffrey's stories about family, about the tension between heritage versus assimilation, and about love, loss, regret, and forgiveness, reveal a sense of absurdity tempered by a love of people and their quirky ways.